THE GIFT
—— *and* ——
OTHER STORIES

WILLIAM H COLES

Copyright © 2024 William H Coles.

All rights reserved. No part of this book may be reproduced, stored, or transmitted by any means—whether auditory, graphic, mechanical, or electronic—without written permission of both publisher and author, except in the case of brief excerpts used in critical articles and reviews. Unauthorized reproduction of any part of this work is illegal and is punishable by law.

ISBN: 979-8-89031-928-9 (sc)
ISBN: 979-8-89031-929-6 (hc)
ISBN: 979-8-89031-930-2 (e)

One Galleria Blvd., Suite 1900, Metairie, LA 70001
(504) 702-6708

CONTENTS

The Gift - 1

The Stonecutter - 19

Facing Grace with Gloria - 31

Homunculus - 41

Reddog - 55

Captain Withers's Wife - 73

The Thirteen Nudes of Ernest Goings - 90

Crossing Over - 112

The Activist - 116

The Perennial Student - 125

Curse of a Lonely Heart - 138

Suchin's Escape - 151

On or more of the stories published in this
volume were finalists or winners in:

William-Faulkner-William Wisdom Competition, Sandhills Writers
Competition, Flannery O'Conner Award for Short Fiction.

THE GIFT

In 1959, a week after her seventeenth birthday, Catherine missed her period in February, and then in March. By late April she was not sleeping well and most of her waking hours were spoiled by nausea and hating everything she ate. Her mother Agnes made an emergency appointment with Dr. Crowder.

"Stay here," Dr. Crowder said to Catherine before he left the exam room. The receptionist had brought Agnes into his private office where she sat in the wing chair for consultations.

"She's pregnant," he said.

Agnes' face paled with the accusation. "She's a child," she said.

How often mothers would not let their children grow up. He gave her time to absorb the truth. "She's a young woman who is going to have a baby," he said.

Agnes wept with her hands to her face. Dr. Crowder handed her tissues from a desk drawer. After some moments, Agnes blew her nose and breathed deeply with a long exhale.

"Have you told her?" Agnes said.

"I've told only you. But she's not stupid."

"Can something be . . . you know . . . done?"

Dr. Crowder stared. He had been the family physician for over thirty years. He had delivered Catherine. "You might find someone. But never ask me, Agnes," he said. "I do not approve."

Agnes flushed. Now she was ashamed. "It will ruin us," she explained.

Bullshit, thought the doctor. Birth is a miracle. Oh, yes. Life was fragile, dangerous, and loaded with inexplicable injustices, but he still loved humanity. And he stayed in practice well beyond retirement to marvel as his patients juggled life's inflated minutia in their own creative ways.

"I'll send her away," Agnes continued.

"Let her make the decision," Dr. Crowder said.

"No. I'll make up an excuse."

"Think about it . . . there would be gossip if she stayed. But if you and Harold were supportive and proud, the gossips would cease caring after a while. And life would go on."

"It's a sin," Agnes said.

"I doubt having a baby is a sin," Dr. Crowder said.

But Agnes could not trust the advice of an idealistic doctor who she thought was immune to reality, nor the judgment of her errant child who was too young and too stubborn to know what her slip-up would do to a prominent family.

At home, to her husband Harold who knew otherwise, Agnes dismissed Catherine's nausea as tummy upset and refused to discuss the baby with Catherine for hours. She blamed Catherine's problem on Harold's family, all of whom were pig-headed and arrogant.

After dinner, alone with Catherine in Catherine's room, she demanded to know the father of the child. She shouted the most likely possibility. But Catherine refused to answer.

"So many you don't even know?" Agnes said.

Then Agnes sent Harold into the bedroom for a one-on-one (she hoped he would beat the crap out of Catherine). Agnes leaned with her ear against the bedroom door so she could hear every word. She was appalled: he was lucky to have a grandchild; birth was God's gift to each of us, and how lucky this baby was to have Catherine for a mother. Not one word of condemnation. It was typical of her husband to turn disaster into a conspiracy against all she had accomplished.

Agnes kept her plan simple. After birth, far away, an immediate adoption was the only solution, and after the town no longer remembered or cared, Catherine could return to live out her penance.

Dry-eyed, Catherine lay on top of her bed covers on her back, which was already the most comfortable position for her. Her father's visit had renewed her confidence. She was a good girl, a girl who made love to only one and with a sincere passion and respect that justified her action. Even with her first suspicions, she could not destroy her lover's future with burdens he could not yet handle. There was virtue in a love baby, far different from sluts who made love to anyone and whores who got paid, a fact she had shouted to her mother when her mother had used the word.

In the days after the doctor's appointment, Catherine endured her mother's frequent side glances and wet hissing sounds, and turned away when her mother reminded her how evil premarital sex was. But soon her mother's unpredictable outbursts became so irrational that Catherine ignored her and turned to prayer for her baby. Her mother then developed a distracting twitch under her right eye, loud speech and short sentences . . . and long cold silences.

In due time, Agnes found the priest, who was hesitant at first to help. Agnes made him admit he had arranged clandestine solutions to similar problems, saying she knew, at least second hand, of a girl he had protected. He soon admitted compliance. He said infant victims of accidental pregnancies deserved a life away from the debauchery of their mothers, who must spend their life seeking fulltime repentance to receive grace. He would help.

Two weeks before school let out for the summer, Agnes took Catherine to the airport. She gave Catherine numbered instructions on a folded piece of notepaper tucked in a paperbound English/French dictionary. Agnes cried briefly at the gate, but she felt only relief when the plane finally took off. She was profoundly afraid of flying, but she felt no apprehension about Catherine's trip; and although she had hated the pain and discomfort of her own pregnancy, she did not worry about Catherine's delivery in a foreign country. Whatever happened, good or bad, Catherine had brought it on herself. All was in the hands of God now. She could not be expected to do more, and she was confident many parents would have done much less, and much less effectively.

The convent school looked like a fortress, with a high stone wall around the buildings that were set next to a wide, rapidly flowing river at the northern edge of the town. In the south of France where the town was located, trees were already full with spring, and the air was warm, even at night. From the hill, visible from the school and anywhere in town, a thirteenth-century buttressed cathedral jutted two spires into the heavens.

The Mother superior was cool and distant but not mean or dismissive, and Catherine, after a few weeks, liked her authoritative efficiency. Catherine began school and attended mass daily, but understood almost nothing. To help, a novice taught her French at private sessions after Matins and after the evening meal.

For weeks, Catherine's sickness came on her at unexpected times. But the Sister in the infirmary gave her medicines and arranged special foods from the kitchen, and soon Catherine felt fine.

Catherine's best friend was Sister Mary Margaret, an impish little nun who rarely thought of God outside of church, but who was eager to be involved with Catherine's delivery of God's gift. Sister Mary Margaret listened to Catherine's fear of dying when the baby came out.

"It is impossible," Sister Mary Margaret said confidently in French, although she had never seen a birth.

"What if God punishes me with a hairy monster?" Catherine said hesitantly.

"God does not always seem to care, but He is not mean," Sister Mary Margaret said.

Then Catherine told her of her fear of being stoned by French peasants—she had seen that in a film, for other sins, with Boris Karloff. Sister Mary Margaret gave her lyrical, bubbly laugh that Catherine loved and frowned as she tried to find the right words in English.

"*C'est fou*," she said.

Agnes did not write, to further emphasize her indignation at her daughter's sin. Catherine sent only rare postcards to her mother, but sent long letters about her new life to her father at the office. Catherine counted the days for her father's return-letters about home that he faithfully wrote.

And Catherine wrote to her priest.

> Dear Father O'Leary:
>
> The Mother Superior speaks English okay and spoke of you at both my meetings with her. She smiles with her memories of when you met. She introduced me to the people who want to adopt. The woman put her hands under my blouse on my bare belly to feel her "*petite poupée*." I didn't like it, but I try to be Christian.
>
> Except for Sister Mary Margaret, one of the nuns, I still can talk to only a few here. The novices laugh when I use French words and they don't try to understand my

English. But I take walks through the town with Sister and visit the Cathedral daily that is half a mile from the school.

The women here sew beautiful clothes they sell in Paris. They have taught me, and I now make baby booties and soft nightgowns for my baby. I crochet lace for the sleeves and the hem, even though Mother Superior says new parents will be waiting to take him . . . or her, away. She says it is best for all that way. As time grows close, I want to keep my baby, but I will not go back on my word.

I help the grounds keeper herd the goats that graze on the lawns of the school. He is a gentle man who sings lively songs in a high voice while he works. He makes goat cheese to give to the poor that tastes awful. But I pretend to like it to please him.

Yours in Christ,

Catti

    When labor pains started regularly, Catherine went to the convent infirmary where there were two iron beds with mattresses. Sister Teresa, the midwife, gave Catherine a draught after the delivery. Catherine slept. When she woke, Sister Mary Margaret sat on a chair next to the bed, her back six inches from the splat. The sheets were clean. Catherine accepted a class of apple cider from her friend. Catherine's body hurt when she rose up to drink. She handed the glass to sister and fell back, exhausted at the effort.
    "Well?' Catherine asked Sister. "Did you see my baby?"
Sister was silent.
    "Was it a girl?" Catherine asked.
    "A little girl," Sister said in English.

Catherine found her friend's hesitancy unexpected, and she turned on the bed to see her friend better. Sister was sobbing.

"What's the matter, Maggie?"

Sister stood up and turned so Catherine could not see her face, then she hurried out the door.

"Please don't go," Catherine called. But Sister did not stop.

Catherine slept that afternoon. Sister Mary Margaret returned in the evening. Catherine was glad to see her.

"I want to see my baby," Catherine said again.

"The baby is gone already."

"So soon?"

"It was Mother Superior's plan."

"What's gotten into you? I thought you were my friend."

Sister Mary Margaret cried again.

"You're useless," Catherine said, immediately sorry when Sister turned her head away. "I want to talk to Mother Superior."

"It is not possible," Sister said.

Catherine threw her feet over the edge of the bed, wincing with pain. "I will go to her," she said.

"No! I will be punished. I was not supposed to tell you."

"Tell me what?"

Sister began crying again.

"What? Tell me, Maggie."

"The baby."

Catherine knew her friend too well to not fear the worse.

"Is the baby dead?" Catherine finally asked.

"Oh, no, not dead."

"What then?"

"She is . . . alive good."

"What is that? What is not right about a baby? Tell me!"

Sister did not speak but squeezed her eyes shut, helping Catherine stand and holding her arm as they went to Mother Superior. Twice Catherine had to sit on benches to rest. Her friend could not speak for her sobs.

"Run ahead. Tell Mother Superior I'm coming," Catherine said. Sister hesitated. "Go," Catherine said, disturbed by her friend's crying.

Catherine was surprised that Mother Superior hugged her for the first time ever, firmly and long. Mother Superior stepped back. "The family would not take her," she said.

Catherine looked to the floor away from Mother Superior. "Why?"

"The baby is not well. They were afraid."

"What is wrong?"

"I didn't see her. But she has no feet."

"That is ridiculous," Catherine said. "I must see her."

"I had the baby sent to a special hospital for children near Lyon. She will be given special care."

"And the parents?"

"They have refused to be involved."

"I must go," Catherine said.

"No. She will have the care she needs to grow . . . and serve Christ."

"I must see her. I will pay the way. Father has sent me more than I need."

"It is not the money."

"I will go. I do not need your blessing."

"You always have my blessings, child."

"I must go too," Sister Mary Margaret said, looking directly into the eyes of Mother Superior.

Catherine used her savings and she and Sister, with the now silent gardener and cheese maker driving, took a wagon to the train station in the next town. With stops, the train took six and a half hours to reach the city. To save money for the return trip, Catherine and Maggie walked two miles from the station to the hospital.

∞

At the hospital, Catherine looked down at the baby, covered in a nightgown. Catherine had already decided her name was Patricia, not Audrey, as the nun dressed in a black and white starched habit had told her. Patricia was in a little nightgown with buttons on the back. One arm in a sleeve waved. The other sleeve partially covered a short arm that ended in three finger stubs that jerked up and out. The nightgown hem lay flat. Catherine retracted the edge. The right leg ended in a smooth knob above where the knee should be. The other leg tapered to an end above where the ankle would be—with no foot. The corner of the baby's mouth tried to smile in a strong effort with unsure results, and the eyes wiggled and waved, sparkling as if sharing the irony of trying to make everything all work right.

"You have seen enough?" the nurse said. Her harsh accent was difficult to understand.

Catherine removed the little nightgown. She smiled at her child, and the child's roving eyes seem to fix on her, at least for a few seconds, until they wandered off, but they came back again. And how soft her skin was, her red hair so fine. Her eyes were faded of color, but inquisitive and sharp. Her lips continued to wiggle at times in an uncoordinated smile.

"She is mine," Catherine said.

"She must stay here with us," the nurse said firmly.

She put the nightgown back on her daughter. She touched the side of her cheek. The little arm waved. She touched the chest with her index finger. There was a little passage of gas with a squeeze of the face.

Searching for French words exasperated Catherine. "Tell her Maggie," she said to Sister Mary Margaret. "Tell her who I am. And get some milk and food for the trip."

Maggie explained in French. The nurse listened intently without response.

Catherine began to take off her sweater to use as a blanket, but the nurse, with a gentle hand on Catherine's arm, let Catherine know to keep her sweater . . . and then wrapped little Patricia in a hospital blanket.

"It is for you," she said in broken English.

When Catherine was holding Patricia against her breast, Sister leaned over and kissed the back of Patricia's head. "*Elle est miraculée,*" she said.

At the convent, every nun and novice were immediately infected with motherly instincts for Patricia. Even the gardener/goat-herder, as the *pater familia*, made daily visits with milk and fresh cut pansies. Sister cooked while Catherine fed Patricia, and she rocked Patricia when Catherine needed rest to regain her strength. And Catherine took Patricia to church, to market, to herd the goats. She sewed, after many trial designs, a special sling that supported Patricia. Patricia was comfortable carried on Catherine's chest or back, and she could face in or out, and sleep when she wanted.

Catherine with Patricia became a common site in town and surrounding fields and wooded paths. Strangers to Catherine waved with pride and familiarity. Catherine loved Patricia's laugh as she jiggled her in the sling; loved her intense stares at new flowers they found in the gardens or in the wild; loved the "ooh" of watching a worm on a stone, or a hawk circling in the sky.

Patricia became adept at getting around the house, using her stumps all together to scurry like a tilted crab. But she was limited outside, and Catherine could see that Patricia would need some upright means of mobility.

Catherine visited veterans who lost limbs in the war, and talked to them about support. They used limbs usually provided by the army, pre-made, and not specially designed. But she learned unique problems for each disability, and studied the principles of various prosthetics. She found a furniture maker and explored different woods—ash and yew and oak—for strong support for Patricia's shorter leg. For the other leg she needed a sturdy foot. At first, a foot replica in walnut was tried; but eventually, a functional design looking like a miniature toboggan, with laminated woods from saplings, was found to be best. Catherine used her sewing skills to attach and brace the prosthetic legs with shoulder straps and snug waste bands. These were attached for stability to the wooden prosthetics by threading through multiple holes. And Patricia, with a laugh, toddled around for a while, tumbling often, and then adapted with the speed of the young, until she could walk, albeit stiffly and with a tilt backward.

This worked for almost a year. But it was not enough. In the leg without a knee, Catherine knew she needed a hinged prosthesis. She wrote Father O'Leary and received a quick response.

> Dear Catti,
>
> I was pleased to discover our own Dr. Crowder went to school with a world authority. Poor Dr. Crowder has had a stroke and cannot walk and he speaks so slowly we can barely understand him. But his mind is sharp, and his wife now writes letters for him, and records drafts he dictates for his memoir. I am sure he would help in any way he can.
>
> God Bless,
>
> Father O'Leary

She received a reply from her letter to Dr. Crowder in two weeks.

Dear Catherine,

How nice to hear from you. You are one of my favorite patients. And I was also glad to hear your little Patricia is saying her first words. I imagine they're all in French, which is a beautiful language.

I do know about artificial arms and legs. But you must come home to see the best. She will need to be refitted often as she grows, and you will have to travel to Boston. But it is a very good idea.

I am a mess with this stroke. But I love my memories.

Sincerely,

Amory F. Crowder.

When Catherine and Patricia left for home, more than a hundred people from the convent and town came to wish them well. Even Mother Superior cried, and Sister Mary Margaret had to be pried away from her hugs of Catherine and Patricia.

Harold and Agnes were at the airport terminal gate when Patricia and Catherine arrived.

Little Patricia took her first look at Grandma and howled.

"Is that any way to treat you grandmother," Agnes said curtly.

"It's not you, mother. The trip has her constipated."

Catherine picked up Patricia and snuggled her on her shoulder, Patricia's footless longer leg poked out below her dress.

"She doesn't look so bad," Agnes said.

"Let me show you mother." Patricia loved to be touched, and loved to be moved. She gurgled with pleasure. "Your grandchild."

"I didn't mean she wasn't perfect."

"*Dis 'bon jour',*" Catherine said to Patricia.

Agnes frowned at the French. Although she thought she knew what it meant, she was always suspicious that there was some meaning in the foreign words that might be against her.

"Say hello," Catherine said, sensing her mother's feelings.

"Lo," Patricia said, and waved her arm at her grandmother, and she smiled. "Lo," she said again.

Agnes gasped at her impulse to reach out and hold her grandchild, and she took back her hands before she had extended them too far, slipping them in the pockets of her sweater.

"Take her," Catherine said.

"Oh, I'll scare her."

"I'll take her," Harold said stepping forward.

Agnes reached out quickly. "I'll do it, Harold," she said.

As Agnes took Patricia, clutching her chest under the arms, Patricia smiled. "Pooh bear," she said with a little spittle.

Catherine handed Patricia a small brown bear with one button-eye missing, and Patricia held it out to her grandmother.

Agnes held her face rigid in resistance to revealing any pleasure. Catherine tensed. But Patricia could not contain her natural affection for people, and she grinned with a warm bubbly sound. Patricia held out her bear again to her grandmother, who smiled, taking the bear and giving it a big hug. Catherine relaxed as her mother jiggled Patricia from side to side, and thanked God for Patricia's magical gift of making others happy.

Agnes held Patricia in her lap on the ride home.

⁂

Patricia discovered Catherine's toys in a trunk and in dresser drawers in Catherine's room that had not been used since Catherine left. Harold had bought a child's bed, but everything else was the same. Agnes found energy she had not had for years: she baked and swept, she arose early before the alarm, and she took daily photos of her family. Catherine got a job as a receptionist in the office of a doctor Dr. Crowder knew. And the newest advances in jointed prosthetics were fitted to Patricia in Boston, and they were awaiting the results any day.

Three times a week, Catherine dressed Patricia in a one-piece red bathing suit she had sewn from a design she had seen in a magazine and took her to the YMCA pool and taught her to swim. Patricia learned to swim quickly, smoothing out her first awkward movements, and Catherine was pleased to think it toned muscles in new ways that Patricia did not normally use and would prepare her for heavier, more complicated prosthetics.

One evening, after Patricia was asleep, Harold and Agnes sat with Catherine in the living room after dinner.

"I don't like you taking Patricia swimming," Agnes said. "People will stare."

Catherine had sensed her mother's disapproval weeks ago. "Why should she not go swimming?"

"It will make her feel different."

"She is different, mother."

"But you shouldn't make her feel bad."

"She has to learn to accept the stares and not feel bad."

"At least you could cover her. That skimpy bathing suit doesn't hide anything."

"That skimpy bathing suit is what most of the children wear."

"But they're different."

"She's not ashamed, mother. She's pretty and very smart. And she has every reason to be proud."

"I didn't mean that, Catherine. Don't twist my words. I just don't want her hurt by those who think her differences should not be exposed. That's all."

"They are curious, mother. People do stare. But for most, it isn't mean and it doesn't last long. And Patricia can be seen for who she is."

"She'll never go out on her own if you keep it up."

"I want her to go out on her own able to handle anything that she might face."

"Be quiet, Agnes," Harold said.

"Don't talk to me like that, Harold. This is important."

"It's not your business. Stay out of it," he said.

"You're always against me. I am not pleased, Harold."

Harold folded his paper, running the dull edge between his forefinger and thumb until it was sharp and then placing it on the footstool. "Take her swimming," he said to Catherine. "Take her everywhere she wants to go."

"That's not what I meant and you know it," Agnes said.

"Be quiet," Harold said as he left the room.

∞

Six weeks later, for Patricia's birthday, they had a party in the kitchen with a cake and candles, balloons and presents. Harold gave Patricia books. Catherine gave her a necklace with a garnet single-stone pendant. And Agnes went to the garage and carried in a small wheel chair with leather seat support and shinning chrome spokes on thick rubber-tired wheels.

"Look at that!" she said to Patricia.

Patricia smiled.

"Can you say thank you?" Catherine said.

"Thank you," Patricia said to her grandmother.

That night, after Catherine heard Harold finish reading one of Patricia's new stories, Pinocchio, to Patricia in bed and she had fallen asleep, Catherine approached her mother in the living room. "You must take the wheel chair back."

"Nonsense. I had it specially made," Agnes said.

"She doesn't need a wheel chair," Catherine said.

Harold came down from the upstairs and sat in his armchair.

"She can't keep up," Agnes said. "I almost lost her in the store."

"She does very well, mother. Just slow down a little."

"The new leg has been good," Harold said.

"She'll be going to school soon. She can't always be strapping on legs," Agnes said.

"She is not a victim, mother. Ignore what she can't do. Help her do what she can."

"How unloving that is, Catherine. How selfish," Agnes said. "You are making her life miserable. You've always been selfish. From the beginning."

Harold's jaws were clenched, and his hands balled into fists. "I will not allow this, Agnes. Take back the chair."

"Ridiculous."

"Take back the chair!"

"It's all right, Daddy."

"No, it's not all right." He stood.

"Don't you walk out on me," Agnes said.

He went into the kitchen. Catherine followed. He had the chair in his hands.

"What are you doing?"

"You're right. She is not a victim, Catherine. I don't want this around."

She had never seen her father this angry.

"I'm taking it to the office for now. Tomorrow, I'll be sure it's returned—or destroyed."

Agnes came into the kitchen as Harold left through the back door, taking the wheel chair to the car.

"Don't you dare . . ." Agnes began.

"Say one more word and I'll explode." He shut the door.

※

Two weeks later, Catherine went to her father's office at the bank during the lunch hour. She had brought sandwiches and sodas for both of them.

"We have to go back," Catherine said to her father.

"Because of mother?"

"We both miss Maggie . . . and all the nuns."

"But it's your mother, isn't it?"

"I hope to find work. But could you help with our trips to Boston?"

"Of course," he said.

They ate in silence for a few moments.

"Your mother loves you both, you know."

Catherine thought for a moment. "She seems ashamed of Patricia sometimes. And she's always been ashamed of me. I don't think shame and love can mix."

It was sometime before he responded. "After I married your mother, I discovered that what she wanted most was to love, but she never knew how," he said while he was stuffing his sandwich wrapper in a bag. "She didn't know what she was searching for. A true disability, I think."

"Do you still love her?" Catherine said.

"She gave me you . . . and Patricia."

They finished eating in silence and then arranged for Catherine and Patricia's return to France within the week.

※

Patricia returned to the States fifteen years later when Catherine, who had established a clothing design business in France that had gained worldwide attention in Paris, moved to New York to expand her designs to the American market. Patricia went to Stanford the same year. She wore knee length dresses or pants when she wanted, her choice made on what was appropriate for the occasion. Harold died of a heart attack, and Catherine and Patricia returned home to visit Agnes on Thanksgiving and Christmas holidays. Pleasant times for all, except for Agnes's silences, smoldering with unstated resentment about how life and her family had treated her unfairly, silences punctuated by biting remarks about how Catherine and Patricia's choice of apparel failed to meet her approval.

THE STONECUTTER

I was thirteen, never in love, and yearning to leave home when a red, two-seated convertible drove up to our gate. The driver's door opened, and a girl of twenty-two with a perfectly shaped, light-skinned body emerged in a see-through dress that showed almost everything, and I imagined the rest.

My father, a tall, imposing figure of a Black man with bulging muscles from carving statues and grave markers for the dearly departed, tried not to look. He felt strange around women, I assumed because my mother had left when I was two. He never talked about her or much of anything, and we lived alone on a twelve-acre plot of half swamp property where I suffered his long silences broken only by the sharp blows of a hammer driving a metal chisel into stone.

Well, this girl was a treat for both of us. She closed the door and looked to our been-here-forever, two-room shack raised two feet off the ground by concrete blocks, with only a screen door on the front and all the windows up to catch a breeze. My father worked on, but slipped a glance when he knew she wasn't looking.

She walked through the opening in the iron fence that stood on the front line of the property. That gate had never kept anything in or out. My great grandfather had installed it in the time of Calvin Coolidge to let people know he had made some cash farming, and my father was too proud to recycle it. Neither the shack nor the fence impressed the girl.

"You lost?" I said walking up to her, smelling the freshness of soap and perfume seeping through the humid air.

"I'm looking for . . ." she turned as if she might go back to the car to find the name.

"Ephraim Picard. Graveyard Stones and Statues?" I said.

"Yes. But I expected . . ." she paused, looking at me with soft deep-water eyes that made me want her so bad I thought I might explode.

"A sign that say the business here?" I said.

"A professional building. Displays of the work."

"Papa don't do things up 'head of time.'"

"I know that. I just expected examples."

"I show you something in the barn might satisfy you some," I said and waved for her to follow. We headed for our barn, not very big and without doors on the front or back so birds flew through without landing. A rusted, out-of-gas forklift half-blocked the door, and I put out my hand for her, which she took, and helped her wobble in her spike-heeled shoes over the two prongs of the fork into the barn.

"Quite the gentleman," she laughed.

Inside on the dirt floor sat blocks of stone and marble randomly stacked, mostly by me. I led her to one corner that was in shadows, but with enough light to see the only sample I could think of showing her. I pulled a tarp off a marble sculpture of a woman's head propped up on two stacked wooden crates.

"Why has it got all those lines through it?" she asked.

"It got smashed," I said. Her hands lightly touched the surface, like a blind person trying to remember someone.

"What happened?"

"Nothing," I said quickly. But Papa had made it and destroyed it.

"Can I see the rest of it?"

I pointed to a rusted tub filled with marble chips, most smaller than an egg from being smashed with a hammer.

"Takes time . . . gluing it back together."

She stood back, walking from side to side to see the whole head.

"Does he always do Negroes?"

"Not always."

"Well, she must be beautiful in person," she said.

"She is," I said, but I didn't really know. I was only two.

"You Ephraim?"

"I'm Willie."

"Well, I'd like to talk to Mr. Picard then."

I led her out of the barn, helping her again over the forklift, but she said nothing about my manners this time.

We approached my father carving a marble angel. She stared. It wasn't a typical graveyard cupid-looking angel made by Italians and chubby with fat as if it couldn't fly. That wasn't Father's way. This angel had a small body with huge muscular wings stretched out on each side: It looked like a hawk in a dive, the smooth-top head cranked back as if catching the full force of the wind, the legs bent back at the knees. My father didn't put clothes on his angels and I wondered what this woman thought about male private parts hanging down.

"You needing something?" Father didn't stop working.

"My father, well, my stepfather, was killed in Statesville, Georgia. At a rally. Maybe you heard of him. Reverend Al Jackson?"

"That was your daddy?" I said.

My father and I had seen The Reverend once in a church we rarely attended up river about a mile. He was campaigning for senator or governor – I don't remember. People yelled and cheered. He had a fat stomach and bulgy eyes, and his solid black capped-toe shoes were polished so they reflected the sun like the mirror-surface of a still pond.

She spoke past me to my father. "His will said he wanted a graveyard statue done by you. He made special arrangements with a cemetery near New Orleans that takes Negroes."

"Takes time," my father said.

"He got special permission from the committee because of who he was, and he wanted it to be bigger than real. Will you do it?"

It wasn't his busiest time, and I thought he'd be eager. But then again, he wasn't a man to jump at anything fast. I, of course, wanted to see this girl as much as I could. With time, I knew I could get her to like me. I was full-grown for fifteen and packed with muscle from lifting those blocks for my father.

She waited for an answer. My father had this infuriating habit of not talking when the silences between him and others clearly demanded some words.

"He do it," I said.

"Will you?" she said to my father.

"Bigger than life takes time," he said again in his deep voice husky from not talking often enough.

"It's in the will I should oversee the progress."

"Why you?" I asked.

"A prerequisite for my inheritance." She added, "Everyday that I come, you'll have to sign and date my book. For the judge."

"I do the writing," I said proudly, "He don't write." Father had worked cane; then he was cleanup boy for a white tomb maker near Lafayette for a while. He learned to carve by watching. I guess he never even thought about school; he'd worked steady and hard his entire life.

"When will you start?" she asked my father. "I need to know when to come back. To keep the terms of the will,"

"Pick the stone tomorrow," Father finally said, still working.

"Not today?"

"You need to bring all his pictures," he said to her.

She sighed and walked back to her car. I ran to catch up with her.

"You miss him?" I asked. "Your step daddy?"

I hated his guts," she said, with so much anger I stopped short. I couldn't think of questions to keep her hanging around, and she got in her car and drove off.

The next day I stayed home from school, eager to be with her, and she brought photos and newspaper cutouts of The Reverend for my father to work from. The sky was heavy with gray clouds and a thin gentle rain came down.

Father led her to the barn; I followed. He waved his hand at the blocks available. She went straight to a slab of marble veined with copper-colored lines the shade of her skin, but my father shook his head and pointed to a huge block of granite.

"I'm supposed to supervise," she said loudly. "I like this one."

"You ain't doing the carving," he said. "That marble ain't big enough."

She walked away fast to let him know she wasn't pleased. Father went back to the angel. She sat on a gravestone already finished and inscribed for a Baton Rouge preacher. I sat down beside her.

"Don't know how to call you, seeing as I'll be the one to do the signing," I said.

"My name is Annatilda Jones. AnnaTee."

"AnnaTee," I said. "He'll make it real good."

"The marble's more elegant," she said sharply.

She didn't know the granite gave power. "You can see the man come out of the big block," I said. "It's cool."

She held her head in her hands. "I can't believe he made me do this," she said.

"The Reverend must of trusted you something hard," I said.

"He was cruel. Arrogant. Thought only of himself," she shot back. "That's why he made me do it."

"What happened to your real daddy?"

"He left my mother early. She was Reverend Al's third wife."

"Me too," I said.

"He's not your real daddy?"

I told her fast it was my mother who had left. And when she asked, I told her how I had never seen her or heard from her.

"You miss your mother?"

"Don't miss her," I said.

The rain came thicker and we moved under the overhang to the barn, away from where Father still worked.

"Why does he work outside?" she asked, her voice soft and friendly for the first time.

"For the light. We ain't got electric out here in the country." Of course, in the seventies, electricity was available everywhere in Louisiana. But my father didn't see a need for it.

"I hope all his statues of people don't come out looking as angry as that angel."

"Naw," I said, "Don't worry." My father was famous for his carving.

Even after a few weeks, AnnaTee didn't gain any interest as to what the Reverend was going to be in stone, but I was like a frog waiting on a fly watching my father finding the man with his hammer and chisel. It is still is a mystery to me how he knew what to chip off and what to leave on.

One day, AnnaTee and I were talking. She was sitting on a rough stone block, leaning back with her hands behind her, her head slightly back; I had my back against the barn wall with my feet out.

"You got a boy friend?" I asked.

When she stared at me, I couldn't tell what she was thinking and my heart dropped like a stone; I'd screwed up. Then she grinned.

"Why are you asking?"

"Just wondering."

"You wouldn't have a crush?" she said with a little laugh.

"I ain't got no crush," I said, but my heart pounded and ached at the same time. I went into the house and sat on the floor next to my bed. I picked notes on a rusty Dobro my uncle had given me, but I couldn't make music. I refused to go out, even when I knew it was time for her to leave.

⁂

I waited every day before going to school to see if AnnaTee would show. I missed her some days when she came late, but not very many. The more time I spent with her, the more curious I became about why she hated The Reverend so much. At the time, I saw hating the Reverend the same as hating God. And I worried about what God's thoughts were about me: The more I spent time around AnnaTee, my shame of my father's ignorance and poverty seemed to keep growing.

"You go to college?" I asked.

"Morehouse."

"What you doing now?"

"Don't know what I'll do. But I was travel secretary for the big man."

"The Reverend?"

"He wasn't reverend. He was base. The whole world was blinded by his smooth tongue." Her anger surprised me again.

"He did good for the ordinary folk. I read it in the paper at school," I said. I had stayed after school to learn about The Reverend. I saw pictures of him with the President, the Secretary of State. In one photo, he had his arm around Martin Luther King.

"He was a crook. He spent the money for the poor."

"I can't believe it," I said. The Reverend was a great man! He had died for all of us. He didn't give a damn about bad people hating him, trying to hunt him down like wild boar.

"His body guards cost a quarter of a million dollars a year! He flew in a private jet that my mother can't sell for a half of what he paid."

"He must have been good to you sometimes!"

"Of course he was good to me sometimes. Of course."

"Then I don't see why you hate him so much."

She glared at me. "You wouldn't know what it means to a woman. He put moves on me! Twice. Even with my mother in the same house thinking he was God's disciple!"

She was shaking, and I felt bad for causing it. I searched for a word to soothe her, but I was lost.

"Maybe he didn't mean it," I said.

"Of course he meant it!" She hung her head and closed her eyes, and I just watched her for many minutes. Then she looked at me, her forehead ridged with lines of determination.

"You don't know about your mother, do you?"

I shook my head.

"Come with me," she said. She was breathing hard, and walked with long strides like she was on a freedom march. She led me straight to Father.

"What happened to the boy's mother?" she said. Father stayed working. "I know you know. Tell him."

The sound of the hammer striking the metal quickened a little.

"She left you, didn't she? She left you."

"Shut your mouth," my father said, moving the chisel to a new sight, starting to strike again even faster.

"You destroyed all this boy had left. Her statue."

"Ain't your doing," he said, his voice seething.

"It's not much to give!" she said. "Ease this boy's longing with the truth."

My father dropped the chisel and raised his hand. I lunged at him grabbing his arm. He shoved me to the ground. I moaned from a pain in my leg.

"Ha!" AnnaTee said, backing away. "Is that what you did? Is that why she left you?"

My father picked up the chisel and went back to working. He was trembling.

"Come," I said, grabbing AnnaTee's arm. I moved her toward her car.

"You'll lose him," she called to my father. "You could at least tell him it wasn't his fault!"

"Don't say no more," I whispered.

She broke away and ran back to my father. "You're evil," she yelled.

My father threw his tools to the ground within inches of her feet, his tight fists at chest high.

"Loosen up. Let the good times roll." Anna Tee laughed.

My father glared. "She loved another," he said.

"Oh! That's so sad. Boo hoo," she said.

"Maybe. Maybe not," he said. Slowly he opened his hands and lowered them to his sides. He headed toward the house.

She hissed. "I hate men," she said as I walked with her back to her car.

⁂

Soon after, AnnaTee stopped coming. She told us she had argued to the court that she had come on and off for three months and that was enough. The judge had agreed. It took Father another two months to finish The Reverend, and when the statue was washed and treated, my father said for me to call and tell AnnaTee when he'd have it installed.

I walked toward the state route, then turned up the levee road to go to Aaron's Shell and Grocery store, where there was a pay phone nailed to an outside pole. I dialed AnnaTee's number and knew her voice when she answered; I'd been cursed to remember it in my lonely times often enough.

"This is Willie."

"Who?"

"Stonecutter's son," I said speaking too loudly. "He's setting it up Tuesday. Doing the unveiling on Wednesday."

"I'll see if I can make it," she said.

Then I called my father's cousin Arno in Morgan City, who hauled trash in a truck big enough to lay the Reverend down for the trip to New Orleans and who owned the unbroken pulleys and intact chains to get him upright again. I skipped school and rode in the truck the eighty miles to New Orleans between Father and Cousin Arno, and helped them bolt The Reverend – after dark – in his final resting place above the tomb, which was no easy task since he was over eight feet high and weighed more than half a ton.

I stayed the night with Cousin Arno's sister-in-law, who lived in the Treme, and I got to walk the streets of the French Quarter.

The next day, Father, Cousin Arno and I went to the cemetery about an hour past sunrise. AnnaTee was there waiting! After a few moments, her mother came, and then friends of The Reverend, and even two crews from TV stations in New Orleans.

The Reverend was covered by six sewn-together bed sheets that were held tight at the base by a rope. A minister of God climbed up on the tomb, with my father's help, to speak about The Reverend, and to God. I went to AnnaTee, who stood off from the crowd a little.

"Hi." It was not what I wanted to say. I wanted to tell her how much I'd missed her, how I wished daily she'd come to see The Reverend – and me. She stared at the fluttering sheets. A breeze gusted, and the sheets flapped.

"You want to see him?" I asked.

"I dread it," she said. I was inches from her, and I could sense how tense she was.

My father walked over to her.

"I brought my checkbook," she said.

"The Reverend Jackson pay me last year he visited. Told me about you."

"He paid you for his statue?" She sounded as if she thought my father was lying. It was all news to me.

"Enough for Willie's college."

"Bought his own monument!" she said mostly to herself, shaking her head.

The minister had finished his words to the crowd, and Cousin Arno cut the fasteners and the sheets fell. AnnaTee's face didn't change one bit. It was like *her* features were in stone.

From a distance, I looked up to the Reverend, standing straight as a tree, his arms crossed over his chest and resting on his stomach. He was in a suit and a tie; his feet, in fancy tassel-shoes, were set together, and were small like his hands. The pale stone made him ghost-like, and at first look, he seemed angry, mostly in the way he stood. But as you studied the lines in his face and his granite eyes that looked down, the anger faded: He showed fear as plain as if he'd been alive and ready to speak. He'd been alone in the world.

AnnaTee felt something too. As if The Reverend himself was talking to her mind. She cried.

I'd had little experience with women, and I turned to Father standing behind us. For the first time I could remember, my father's face softened and his mouth turned up a little, not much at all, but a lot for him, and like a bolt of lightning from a grey sky, I was proud of him. Proud of his work. Proud what he'd done for The Reverend, who was, as promised, bigger than life. And for AnnaTee, who had her inheritance. I smiled back.

"What you think?" I said to AnnaTee.

She didn't try to speak for a minute or so. "It's so big. I think that's what hit me."

"I think he was a great man," I said.

"It's not what I expected to feel," she said. Her face softened with a little less hate than before.

Then she hugged me, long enough for me to hug her back. "You're sweet, Willie," she said. "You'll do just great in college."

Being sweet wasn't at all what I wanted to hear, but I formed an immediate plan. I would stay with my father on the property until I finished school. I would grow up and be educated. AnnaTee would learn to love me.

But the truth still hurts, even after these many years. Papa died when I was in college, and the letters I wrote to AnnaTee came back unopened. I never saw her again.

FACING GRACE WITH GLORIA

I was sleeping in this mission after being discharged from the psych ward at DC General, and some hophead stole my cash from my veteran's disability checks that had piled up while I was so rudely and unjustly incarcerated. So I dropped by my best buddy, Arthur, who lived in two side-tilted Dumpsters at the edge of inner Washington, DC.

"You got any cash?" I asked.

"Nothing."

"I want to visit my mother."

"She write to you?"

"Not yet. But she needs me. Came to me when I was inside."

Mother was in Eureka, California. At least her spirit was, and her ashes were, too, in an urn in my older sister's bungalow; I hoped they were out of reach of her two young children by her second husband. My sister refused to see me, but Mother cared that I came to visit. I slept in a cardboard lean-to near Route 1, and I could feel Mother in the air, even when it rained.

"I need money," I said.

"Work the monument," Arthur said.

"That'll take weeks."

"Hey. You might get lucky."

I cleaned up best I could in the restroom of a discount trade mart, and headed on down to the Potomac River.

I put my cardboard sign up on an intact discarded painter's easel: "Crash site. Tours. Flight 63. $1.00. Kids free." I waited.

A few folks dribbled by but they gave me wide berths and blank stares. After an hour three ladies came up – I'm blessed, from my mother's side, with a right-on feeling about people – and I knew at least two of these broads were trouble: cranky oldies who were dressed, one in brown the other in gray, like spinster twins, in ankle-length dresses with long sleeves, probably from a Midwest town too small to have a library. These were women who cut their own hair without looking in a mirror. But the third was a girl, maybe nineteen-or twenty-years-old. She had even-edged shoulder-length hair and a round face like one of those angel paintings by Italians you see in the gallery near the toilets in the museum on a free night. She wore this short skirt that didn't cover her cute little knees – all puckered with dimples and curves like little midgets laughing. And she moved as if she had no weight. Her name was Gloria.

They paid their three bucks; I'll give them that. I took them to a riverside grove of trees that hid the shrine that was a waist-high pyramid of round and oval rocks worn smooth and cemented together. Some rocks were gray or brown, but others were dried-blood red or almost white. A few glittered with mica. On top, I had supported with loose stones a plastic yellow flower with a red center and green leaves on the stem.

"The plane came down right over there." I pointed to the river, very wide at this point. We were in comfortable shade, now, about seventy-five yards from the bridge.

"You saw it crash?" Brown said.

"Yep."

The gray lady scowled. "Liar! We had loved ones on that flight. It went down nine miles from here."

"I take exception," I said firmly. "Plane came down late fall." I told them about the pregnant woman and all the little children.

"We must insist you discontinue this scam."

I took out two pictures of the crash and rescue from my pocket. Each was a newspaper clipping laminated with drugstore plastic and trimmed to fit the hand. But they ignored my photos.

"What exactly is *that*?" said Brown nodding at the shrine.

"A shrine to a man who sacrificed himself for another," I said with the genuine pride Arthur had taught me. "You want to take a free picture? You'll never see another one like it."

"Using a tragedy to make money," said Gray. "Disgraceful."

"We're in Washington for a settlement," brown lady said. "We were appalled by your sign."

"You must stop," Gray sputtered.

"I've already settled," said the girl.

Wow! This might be luck.

"A shrine to honor a real hero," I said, pulsing to the potential, looking directly to the girl, watching those eyes for the faintest touch of sympathy for the dead. I saw the flash of caring!

The other two glared on.

"You're lying to people," said the girl.

"I was there! A little upstream," I admitted. "But I saw it."

"You're sick," the girl said, not with hate, but sad. Real sad. And her eyes shifted – washed with a cringe of fear I often see – as if I were a lunatic. Well, the last shrink I saw thought I was bi-polar. She was a medical student and I said, "It's schizophrenia, doc! We're like Mensa, Harvard Divinity and Yale Law. Not lazy and not crazy. A disease of the genes!" But the doc shook her head and said I had a lot to learn. You can see my conundrum. Gloria had cash to give but she had no respect for me, and I just wasn't clear on how to tap her reserve; but I was clear that this wasn't the group to pass our best moneymaker to - my red-painted shoebox with the slot in the top for donations to the families' "relief fund."

I followed them back to the bridge. My heart sank as they walked away. At the other side of the bridge, the girl said something to the two oldies, broke away, and returned to me as the others walked on.

Some driving need had overtaken her; I could see it in her walk. Up close, she stared as if I were some mysterious gift wrapped up in twice-used Christmas wrapping. I was panting with the possibilities for a trip to Eureka. And she was so pretty! She brought a flood of happiness like too many suds in a bubble bath.

"You really were at the crash," she said. "One of the flight attendants was pregnant. She told me herself. But no one knew."

I let her believe.

"What month?" she asked.

"February."

"Day?"

"Fourth."

"I mean day of the week."

"Monday." All that was in the clippings.

"I was there!" I said with conviction. "Me and my buddy were sleeping in a crevice under the bridge. It's been filled in now."

"Oh, no!" She started sobbing. "You weren't really there." She slipped down into a crossed-legged position like a monk. I couldn't bend like that so I stood and tilted over a little bit. Nothing came into my head so I let her weep it out.

"I know that bridge. There was no place for people to sleep. I know every inch. I thought you might have really been there, in spite of all these lies."

I tried to hold back, but something about this sweet innocent thing reminded me of Mother and told me it was time to paint a little truth. It wasn't easy.

"I wasn't there," I said. "Only Arthur, my buddy was there. But he's real sick and waiting on word from a class action suit on Agent Orange. So I'm the only one to honor the hero. He told me every detail."

I decided not to tell her that Arthur, who glued the rocks onto government property, believed he'd seen the miracle face of God the night of the crash and did these shrine tours for free for years, passing a hat for donations of course. He began charging when his cough-spit turned red and he really needed doctor-cash.

She didn't look surprised. Just disappointed. "I wish you had been there," she said. "I want to know about the man. Can I talk to Arthur?"

This was where experience counted.

"Arthur is a loner. Keeps his peace, mostly," I said, my head down and not looking at her.

"Is he here? In the city?"

"He's on the edge."

"I want to talk to him."

"I can't take the time," I said turning away. "I've got to stay the day."

She grabbed my coat sleeve near the patch. "I'll pay. I've got money."

"No way."

"Please take me?"

She reached in her purse and peeled off two tens from a roll of bills—a *big* role of *big* bills.

Owwee! But I shrugged with disinterest. She added two more.

It's cash from the crash, I thought. Probably more than she needs.

Then she peeled off two, three, four . . . biggies!

"Okay!" I said. "But the cab's on you."

I grabbed the flower and my laminated shots, slipped my sign in my plastic trash bag, grabbed my easel, and we were on our way.

The cabby dropped us off two blocks from Arthur's abode. The cabby said he didn't drive into the valley of sure death for anyone.

"We can walk," Gloria said brightly. A sweet girl totally unafraid and unaware this wasn't Main Street, USA. Sure enough, on the way I saw human movement in the shadows of an abandoned warehouse, and I grabbed her arm and hustled her along so she never knew.

Near a landfill, she stared in wonder at Arthur's two discarded Dumpsters tipped on their sides, angled like the open jaws of a dinosaur skeleton's head, and covered with tarps and cardboard sheets held down with rocks and bits of concrete. He had a discarded Porta-Potty, with no door, out back. He was asleep, sitting up in his aluminum chair, with tubes curving under his arm and over his chest and plastic wraps over his oxygen tanks.

"That's him," I told my new friend.

"Is he alive?"

Arthur coughed in his half-sleep. Then he gave up a wet one.

"Don't stand too close. You get hit with the spit."

She moved back a step.

"Arthur," I said. "Meet and greet. You got company."

Arthur shook his head so his gray-streaked beard wagged like a broom on front. He was wearing only shorts and torn sandals with straps and soles smoothed by some long-gone hippie. Sweat glistened on his forehead.

Although he was half-blind, I waved my cash behind her as she stared at him, trying to get him on board my Gloria train. Arthur didn't have my instincts for the big deal.

"You were at the crash? Air Florida 63?" she gushed. Arthur missed my cash wave behind her head.

"Why do you ask?"

"My father was on that flight. Flight 63."

Arthur finally saw me and gave me a glare. I put away the cash. "Sorry about your dad," I said.

"I'm having a little trouble understanding your purpose," Arthur said.

"I saw the shrine. I thought you saw the crash!"

"A hero," Arthur said.

"Tell me. I want to know!"

Arthur coughed as if to get the story spirited into his voice. He pushed up in his chair and leaned forward slightly. He'd told it before. The DC bard, he was. This was going to be great!

"It was just before midnight, wet snow coming down almost like rain. The jet had iced wings and lost altitude after takeoff. The pilot tried to land on river ice to miss people on the ground. The plane slid on its belly and stopped. Survivors crawled out the exits and slid into the frozen river grasping for anything – but there was only ice. The plane sank, slow at first, then faster. Like the Titanic."

"In the Atlantic," I said.

Arthur ignored me. "Poor souls lost, some bodies never found."

"What about the man?" she asked.

"The rescue chopper arrived and let down a line with a clamp. It wasn't a chair or anything fancy. The man grabbed the line and could have saved himself but he turned to a woman – a stranger I learned later – holding onto a piece of ice about fifty feet away. The man shoved the line toward her but the chopper downdraft blew the line away. The man pointed at the line; it stopped in midair. With a slow motion of his hand he willed that line to move to her. 'Strap it around your chest' he yelled, 'Under your arms! Snap the clamp!' The chopper-people pulled that woman into the aircraft, a spotlight still fixed on this man who was glowing like a light bulb filament. I watched him. The rotor air wash splashed water on the ice and he couldn't hold and he went under. The chopper flew off."

"A miracle," I said.

"A tragedy," Arthur added wisely.

"Could you see him?" the girl asked of Arthur.

"Yeah. I was maybe two hundred feet away."

"Was he old?"

"What do you mean, 'old'?"

"Fifty?"

"Yeah. I could see his face. About fifty."

"Could you see his hair?"

"Like the color?"

"Was he bald?"

"Bald. I could see he was bald," Arthur said.

The girl eyed Arthur as if he had just parted the Red Sea. I thought that was a good sign for closing the deal, sort of just payment for the true scoop.

"He was a big man," Arthur said.

"With big shoulders?"

"It was hard to know with him in the water. But I could tell by his neck he was large."

"He was a big man!" she said as if in a dream. Then the kid started crying.

"Your father?"

She nodded.

"A son of God."

"He died for a stranger," I said. "A real hero!"

"To do that for another human being," Arthur said., "A man blessed with the grace of God." I thought Arthur had gone too far bringing the grace of God into it.

She wiped her nose with the short sleeve of her blouse. "I didn't know my father well. My folks were divorced and I lived with my mother. She says it couldn't be my father who saved that woman."

Arthur let go with a lung-turner of a cough. His face turned red. The bald dome on top of his head flushed. "That's the story," he finally said.

The girl dug in her bag. She wanted to give Arthur five of her big bills. Behind her back I gave Arthur a one-man high-five. Crazy Arthur said "no." He'd never accept anything from the daughter of *him*, he said. Goddamn! Arthur had always been a little slow to embrace opportunity, but this was ridiculous.

Gloria sat motionless for a while. Her wad must have had a thousand dollars. Just a little of that would make an easy round-trip bus ride to Eureka, if added to what I had. I felt like bawling. When she had collected herself, she thanked Arthur again, said she was grateful to know.

"Walk her down to that motel near the expressway. They'll call her a cab," Arthur instructed.

I protested but Arthur had fallen asleep again.

We were on our way – me, and Gloria, and her cash.

"What's Arthur's last name?" Like she might send him a thank you note or a little gift in the mail.

I wasn't feeling up to chatting. "I'm not sure. O'Leary, maybe. I forgot his lot."

"Will he die?"

"I ain't a doctor. But he looks dead already."

We walked without talking. She had a new spring to her stride. She was smiling to herself, as if someone had given her warm cocoa on a cold night. I hate children, but if I had to have one, I'd have chosen Gloria.

We were close to the motel. She stopped, opened her bag and asked if I needed more. Maybe not all was lost. I could make it to Eureka, and maybe get Arthur out of the VA clinic to a real doctor, too.

"That's a lot of dough," I said, eyeing her stash.

"You've been so kind." She offered me at least five hundred.

I was fighting with myself inside. More money than I'd seen in years. Maybe I wouldn't tell Arthur; he would never know, and I deserved it after all I'd been through to set it up. Ideas were bouncing around in my head like Ping-Pong balls in a rotating lottery cage. One crazy idea kept popping up! If she did pay, she would soon wonder if Arthur's story was true and whether it was really her dad or not.

"It's yours," she said.

I shook my head no in a moment of insanity. I just wasn't up to erasing Arthur's graffiti from this girl's blackboard.

The sun was gone, rubbed out by a rain cloud, and the roar of an eighteen-wheeler downshifting blasted us from the overpass of the expressway. I saw her to the motel lobby sliding door that was stuck on closed and I pried it open for her. I turned quickly. There was no need for long good-byes.

HOMUNCULUS

Didi sits on a three-legged stool on the stage in a sideshow tent. It's the third show of the night. She listens to the barker, Captain Withers, as he gathers a new crowd outside. "Didi, the Dynamic Dwarf! The doll of the midway!"

On stage, Didi is hidden behind the wooden façade of a miniature house with a hinged door and two fake windows and an angled roofline bent on each side of the peak. The tent air is hot and stuffy, and sweat trickles from her armpit down her side. She wonders if it is due to nerves or the weather.

"This tiny morsel – born of ancient royal heritage – is the reincarnation of Cleopatra, an Egyptian goddess. The smallest woman in the world. Thirty-two inches low. You will see every detail, of God's amazing work. Right here, tonight, gentlemen, and for two nights only."

Didi's real name – Gloria Pinkham – is rarely used, a smudged memory from the real world. After eight years with the circus, she barely remembers the shape of her mama's house on a side street in Lewiston, Maine. She carries a scratched daguerreotype of her mother sitting in a chair; her father, stiff as a cigar-store Indian, stands by her side with a hat in his hand. The war killed him when Didi was four; he faded away in some Georgia prison. He left her no memories.

Captain Withers yells until he fills the first four rows of the twelve benches with customers. Didi doesn't care how many; she gets food, shelter, and a few dollars every month if there are two, ten or twenty.

These farmers and farmers' boys are like fish in a pond – different sizes and hard to tell apart. They've never been more than twenty miles from their mothers or wives, and they clump together like curdled cream to gawk at something from away. She sees in their gaze how they undress her, their curious glares often speckled with desire. She loves to be wanted and she wants to be loved. But she hates pity; when she sees it in a sucker's eyes she looks away and pretends it's not there.

Captain Withers signals those inside when he yells, "You're lucky, my friends, the show is just starting," and blows his whistle. Didi opens the hinged door in the house facade and steps out onto a stage that dances with the shadows of four flickering torches. Wisps of smoke cloud the air. Growls, shrieks and cries pulse from the midway and dampen the scattered applause. The eighteen-by-twelve foot stage with collapsible support beams rises three feet above the ground. The front is slightly lower than the back, and there is barely enough room for the miniature dogcart in front of the dollhouse façade. To make Didi look smaller, the cart has oversized wheels and a single seat on a small frame. Didi mounts the single step, sits on the seat and waves. She wants them to enjoy her. She watches the faces of the men and boys with the same intensity as they watch her. Men mystify her. Didi wants a husband to pamper, children to correct, a house to come home to even if it is just during the winter when the circus doesn't travel. She dreams of Lazlo the Hungarian trapeze artist.

Rudy, the Daring Dwarf, handles Terry the Terrier, who is harnessed in front of the cart. With a leash, Rudy leads the dog through a tight figure-eight journey around the stage. Then Didi steps down. Rudy picks up a half-sized banjo from behind the house facade and strums. Didi sings a song – "Wandering in the Garden of My Mother's Withered Roses." When Rudy signals with his hand, Terry wags his tail. Didi unhooks her gown and it falls away; Rudy dashes to collect it. Terry barks. Didi wears a see-through costume over white under garments that resembles a nightgown and glitters with sequined trim. Her breasts swell in the golden silk of the fabric. Didi pulls up the hem, shows her baby-like ankle, part of her stubby leg. She climbs back into her dogcart carriage holding her nightgown so that much of her backside is exposed. Seated, she crosses her legs so her dress rides up her thighs and Rudy comes over and kisses her on the cheek. Off they go. Off the stage. Behind the facade. The act takes less than five minutes.

As Rudy and Didi leave the stage, Billy Batton, the full-size sideshow buffoon, walks up and down the rows of spectators whispering, "You want to see Didi's thing? Her woman stuff? Over there." Billy collects additional money and points to the tent flap where gentlemen go, one at a time, into a booth the size of a one-hole outhouse. In the dark, a two-inch diameter hole glows weakly from candle light on the other side. It's on the back wall, about four feet above the ground, and easy to find.

With one eye pressed to the hole, a customer sees Didi's feminine parts. They are perched on a table covered with purple-red velvet drapes mounded to suggest that Didi is lying on her back with her knees raised and her legs spread apart. The edge of the drape can't quite cover a little piece of gold cloth with sequins – the same cut of cloth as Didi's gown. Between the two leg-mounds is a slit the size of the spine of a small hymnal that reveals moist flesh poorly illuminated by two candles in glass hurricane shades on a side table. These are really the private parts of a freshly killed lamb.

In the dressing tent, Didi is folding up her white dress to place it in the trunk with her golden gown when Captain Withers grabs her by the arm. "Tell Rudy one more show."

"We ain't finished?"

"You talk too much for a runt."

Didi wishes Captain Withers would drop dead. She hates his voice. She hates his yellow teeth and his breath that stinks like the floor of a chicken coop. And she hates what he makes up about her. About her savage beginnings. About how all the dwarves crave her. And she's thirty-four inches, not thirty-two. One time in Indiana, when Didi tried to run away to marry a barber's son, Captain Withers whipped her.

Rudy stamps his feet when she tells him about the show. It's something a full-grown man wouldn't do, and she feels embarrassed for Rudy – and for herself. "It's not fair," he says.

"Of course it's not fair. It's not fair being some shrunk-up freak either."

After the last show, Rudy helps Didi fold her costumes. He walks her back to the wagon where six of the thirteen circus dwarves sleep. Rudy touches Didi's bare arm and tries to hold her hand, but she takes it away.

"Let's get out," he says. "You and me."

Didi laughs. He is a funny little man, always dreaming the impossible. His only skills are making Terry the Terrier do its tricks and making people smile with his curious thoughts. And he wants to hold her in the night, he says, forever, and keep her warm when the drafts sneak through the boards of the wagon.

Rudy stops her near the utility wagon. He grabs her shoulders and turns her small body toward him. His wide face is round with teeth that are too big and lips too small to hide them. His eyes are wide apart and give him a dull-witted look, although Didi knows he is very smart. He writes letters for her, and reads the ones that come from her mother.

"I'm going. With or without you."

"Poof," says Didi.

"I mean it."

"Where would you go?"

"I'll figure it out."

"And you'll starve. You'll be eaten by wolves."

"You'll see," says Rudy. Didi hears a resolve in his voice. Would he really leave without her? She has assumed that he will always be there for her, always leading her wagon. But she says nothing, and they turn to climb the small closely spaced steps into the wagon where four dwarves play cards and a fifth is playing "Oh! Susanna" on a harmonica, a sweet and lively tune that makes Didi happy and sad at the same time. "It rained all day the day I left, the weather it was dry ... Susanna, don't you cry."

That night Captain Withers dies. He does not drop dead exactly, but he is found on his cot in his wagon, twisted at the waist, his legs in a grotesque pose of writhing. Most circus people think it was some sort of fit. He's lost all control of his bowels and bladder and snot hangs out his nose. With her low vantage point, Didi gets a direct peek at dead Captain Withers' open eyes. He looks afraid. She whimpers to impress the other circus people who are near, but she wants to laugh and clap at the same time.

"He did the best he could," says Rudy.

"You're crazy," says Didi. A crew from the animal wagons takes Captain Withers out near the river and buries him and his soiled nightclothes in a damp shallow grave. Some sideshow people watch; Didi doesn't go, but Rudy tells her, and she worries that the hasty grave is too shallow to bury the mean spirit of Captain Withers. She dreads his image in nightmares, and fears wicked spirit visitations from his black soul. She asks Rudy about the grave.

"Graves don't matter. I'll take care of you," he says. But Didi wants Lazlo the trapeze artist, not Rudy. And she doesn't want the ghost of Captain Withers to haunt her.

The next morning the new barker, Colonel Phister, who is part owner, starts to make changes. "To not go broke," he says, "not to belly up." He does not like Didi's act. "Never have," he says. He wants an act that will make the farmers and their boys come back the same night to see it, as he puts it, "again." Pay more money. At first Didi is excited; she dreams of a better position on the midway, with new costumes. But Colonel Phister wants to double bill her. "We'll make more money with the giant," he says.

"Gargantuan does his own act," Didi complains.

"He's a dud. There ain't no surprise. No one pays to see a giant in a tent when you can't miss seeing him outside on the midway. We got to do something original."

Colonel Phister thinks Gargu the Giant should be the one to unloose Didi's dress. Fumble a little. Build some tension.

"What about the dog?" Rudy asks.

"No dog. Just play that goddamn banjo. And change that stupid song. Get one of them nigger tunes."

Gargu the Giant is slow to think. "Why you want to change the act?" he asks when he looks down on Didi, Rudy and Colonel Phister. Didi thinks if she's got to share billing, she'd rather it be in the big tent with Lazlo.

"I could work with Lazlo and the trapeze family."

"That's stupid. Ain't no runts in the big tent."

"We work with the clowns," Rudy replies.

"That's different," says Colonel Phister.

"Can't we wait for winter quarters?" says Didi. "Take some time to work things out?"

But Colonel Phister sees economic potential. "Now," he responds. They change the act on the road. Didi has new billing: "GARGU the GIANT and DIDI the DYNAMIC DWARF with Rudy the Daring Dwarf playing BANJO."

They decide to have Didi enter on the dogcart after all, but do away with the dollhouse facade that needs painting anyway. When Gargu the giant tries to pick up Didi, he grips her waist so hard she cries out. She refuses to let him touch her. So they get an eight-rung little ladder that they prop against Gargu's chest. Rudy holds the base of the ladder steady. Didi climbs up, and when she is almost to the top, Gargu kisses her and puts her on his shoulder. Rudy takes the ladder away. It is from there, holding onto Gargu's hair on the back of his head for support, that Didi sings her new song, "Oh, Susanna."

"The sun so hot I froze to death...Susanna, don't you cry."

Colonel Phister wants Didi to show her body. He gives her a shorter see-through gown and he has Gargu hold her up and look up under her dress. "Make 'em want to pay to see," Colonel Phister says. To dismount from Gargu's shoulder, Colonel Phister thinks Didi needs to have a whiz-bang ending. "Jump."

"I'll kill myself," Didi protests.

"We'll borrow a trampoline from the Wondrous Polenskys."

"You can't make her jump. It's too dangerous. She's the star," says Rudy to Colonel Phister.

"She ain't no star. She's a runt on the midway."

Because the Polensky trampolines are too big for the stage, Colonel Phister has the carpenter build a circular wooden frame with a diameter the size of two barrelheads and stretch a canvas over the top. Didi jumps to fall on her back and spring up so she lands on her feet on the stage. She can't get the timing right, and she bounces crooked and lands in a heap.

"That's great," laughs Colonel Phister. But it hurts to fall wrong and Didi practices every day to get it right. She jumps off the water wagon onto the new special dwarf trampoline to practice landing on soft grass. Then she climbs back up an iron ladder bolted to the side of the wagon and jumps again. And again. Until she can land standing up almost every time.

Rudy is a pest. He finds flowers in the fields or next to the rivers, and brings them to Didi to celebrate the new act. In the mess tent, he offers part of his apple pan dowdy to Didi. He says he loves her. She smiles at his passion, but thinks he is short and ugly. She is ashamed of him; he is a joke of a man no one could love. And she resents his advances because he could never be Lazlo the Hungarian trapeze artist.

Lazlo wears white tights trimmed with sequins. Although he is barely five feet tall, he has wide shoulders and strong arms that hang down, each bent like a tightly strung bow. On each arm, a bicep bulges big as a potato. His black hair is cut short, and his small ears are low on his skull. His eyes are dark and close together. He is clean-shaven except for a thin mustache, and he has a big smile and good teeth that are only a little uneven in spacing. He flies through the air and the crowds hush so that Didi fears they might hear her heart racing. Every unmarried girl likes him. A lot of marrieds too. Many give themselves to him hoping he will marry them. Didi knows that Khatooma the Cat Woman and Rhonda, who is second billing for the Flying Rolands' horse riding act, both had to get their babies stopped. Lazlo's babies.

Didi is sure that Lazlo could love her if he knew her. Big people have loved little people. She's heard of long, happy lives together. And Lazlo isn't that big. He just needs to get to know her. And isn't she pretty? Doesn't she have long hair that flows to her waist? He could comb it for her. She could sew his costumes. They could have a house somewhere with china plates.

She has a plan. She hopes to talk to Lazlo alone, as if by accident. She will meet him after a show when he is going back to his family's wagon. She is smaller than a wagon wheel so that she can fit under many wagons without bending. She waits hidden in the shadow of the tent-pole wagon every evening for a time when Lazlo might walk by alone on his way from the main tent. For two nights, he is with someone. Then the third night he is alone, and she pops out and acts as if she is walking the other way.

"Hi, Lazlo. You did real good tonight."

"You think so?" Lazlo says. And he smiles. "You're mighty cute down there on the edge of center circle," he says. When she goes back to wagon where the dwarves sleep, she smiles to herself and hums her new tune, "Oh, Susanna."

Each night, Didi goes back under the wagon to wait for accidental time with Lazlo. When Didi and Lazlo are alone, she tells him how accomplished he is, and she makes him laugh with stories about little Rudy and Rudy's silly ways.

In the tent where Madame Fortuna does her séances to talk with the dead, Didi climbs into the red velvet upholstered chair used for soul seekers. Madame Fortuna is Didi's big friend, and Didi talks to her often about Lazlo, about making a family.

"I love him," Didi says.

"Ah, vat eeze luf?" Schenectady-born Madame says in her European accent that Didi wishes she could learn. Didi practices alone, away from the others, dreaming she might have a real speaking part in the act some day. Lazlo has an accent.

"I want to be his wife."

Madame Fortuna takes off her turban and shakes out her thin hair. It is black, streaked with gray. Hidden in a wash of French perfume, Didi smells a mixture of sweat, mold, and dead shellfish.

Didi tells her about her meetings with Lazlo.

"You've got to make him want you," Madame Fortuna says.

Didi thinks for a moment. "He likes me. I know it."

"He's got to crave your body. Wake up in the night hot for your wares."

"You mean down there?" Didi nods to her private parts.

"Do you know a man can fit?"

"I've heard."

Madame Fortuna unties the sash that holds her robe. Her large breasts hang loose, ballooning her undershirt. "I mean did you make love to a big man? Did it work?"

Didi doesn't speak. She does not want to say she has never made love to any man. Big or small.

"Being with a man hurts me, Didi. And I ain't small by a long shot."

Didi squirms in her chair. She believes that when you love someone it can never hurt.

Madame clears her throat. "I'd forget it."

"I can do it," Didi blurts out.

"Look, honey, don't get mad. It just ain't possible."

"I'm a real girl. It ain't just lamb parts."

"Well, he's had every girl who would let him. He'd be glad to add you. With women, he's like Bill Cody shooting buffalo."

"I know he's not like that."

"He's an uncaring bastard, Didi. The worst kind of man."

"I could make him want me," Didi mumbles.

Madame Fortuna has not said what Didi wanted to hear. Now Didi thinks Madame is too old to know of these things about love, although she has been helpful before. Does she have a man? No. Besides, her tealeaves are tobacco, and she smells bad.

Didi is so angry with Madame Fortuna, she goes directly to Lazlo. She finds him practicing on a bar propped between wagons. Didi says she needs to talk to him.

"Of course." He smiles.

"Alone," says Didi.

Later that night, she meets him behind the laundry wagon. She is there early and he comes late. He slides down on the grass beside her and sits with his ankles crossed and his knees apart.

Didi tells him about the new act. She talks about Captain Withers dying before she says, "Do you think I'm pretty?"

"Exquisite," Lazlo says, and smiles down into her eyes.

"Could you love me, Lazlo?"

"I love you. Naturally." His accent seems thicker now.

"Really love me. Like a wife?"

"Ah. That is the question?"

"Of course it's the question, you oaf. It's what's important to me."

"You're a very pretty woman."

"But I'm too small." Didi pouts.

"No, you are very attractive. Desirable."

Didi takes his hand, feels the calluses on his palm, rough like cured leather and harder than amber. "Make love to me, Lazlo."

"Here?"

"No. We'll go over near the edge of the woods."

Lazlo squats to look into Didi's face. "You mean it?"

Didi nods. She looks up into his eyes. He still grins, but she is sure he is not making fun of her. He seems interested. Curious, maybe. She wonders – wasn't this what she wanted? She reaches out to put her finger on his lips. She feels the scratch of his waxed mustache.

"It is not possible?" Lazlo asks.

"Of course it is. I've known lots of small people who love big people."

"We must be quick."

"Of course."

"Be sure no one knows."

"Absolutely."

"I'll get a blanket," Lazlo says.

"Yes. Hurry," she says.

As Didi waits, Lazlo finds a washed blanket on a line strung between two wagons. It is dark among the wagons, and he touches the blanket's lower edge to see if it is dry. He yanks it off the line. Together they walk. Didi hurries to keep up. He reaches down and grabs her by her shoulders. Lifts her.

"Put me down."

Lazlo laughs. He walks a little faster. Didi twists out of his grip, sputtering, and when she is free she has to trot to keep up.

Lazlo finds a dark spot and throws the blanket onto a grassless patch of dirt under a tree. There is a late quarter moon and a faint glow from the cooking fires from the circus. She sees the mussed blanket. From each corner she works to the center and smoothes it as best she can.

Lazlo has taken off his pants. Didi looks away, embarrassed and afraid, and sees the low branch of a tree move. It could not be the wind.

"Lie down," she says.

"No. You." He still has on a tight shirt. He has kicked off his slippers.

She fears his weight. Her bones are easy to break. "I can't." When he bends slightly, she thinks it is to find his pants to leave, and she is surprised that she feels relief. But Lazlo moves his pants off the blanket and lies down on his back. His member looks different – still hard, but pointing to his chin and pulsating a little. Didi smiles because it looks silly.

She takes off her dress, but keeps her shoes on. She presses her palms together to keep from shaking. She pulls her undershirt overhead and stands next to Lazlo, who is looking at the stars with his hands locked behind his head. She straightens her back so her breasts jut out a little more, and she moves a few steps toward him.

Lazlo reaches up and touches her left breast, scratching her nipple with his rough skin. Didi senses his disappointment as he pulls away his hand. Did he expect more?

She reaches over to take his organ in her right hand. Her stubby fingers can't get around it so she uses both hands. It is warm, but not as hot as she expected. And she can feel the surge of Lazlo's heart pumping the blood into his organ. "Damn it. Be careful," he says.

"What happened?"

"It's tender sometimes," he says. "Ain't you had it before?"

Didi wonders why she feels dread instead of excitement. She tries to touch Lazlo carefully, standing next to him, barely needing to bend. She strokes his member with the tip of her finger.

"You jump on," he says.

"Do you love me?" Didi says. But he doesn't answer.

She strokes him a few more times and he moans. He breathes hard. He tries to grab her breasts, but he can't get a hold of the little mounds. He grips her arm, draws her closer to him. His member is still between her palms, and it squirts like a cannon – three times she thinks, but maybe four. She is so surprised she squeezes. He swats her hands away.

"I didn't ..."

"Shit," says Lazlo.

She wipes her hands on her hip, then picks up her nightshirt and cleans off each finger of her left hand.

Didi tries to take his hand, but he jumps to his feet, puts on his pants, pulls the blanket from under her so fast she tumbles down, hurting her shoulder.

"Lazlo," she says softly, but he is too far away to hear. "Lazlo."

She stays on the ground, rolls onto her back in the same position Lazlo waited for her. She rubs the sore shoulder until the pain is dull. She looks to the sky and the stars. Follows the outlines of the Big Dipper and Orion's belt. Some stars twinkle in pairs, like eyes watching. In a few minutes, she is cold, and she rises to put on her clothes. Then she lies back down, still chilled, but not wanting to return to the cluster of wagons and tents. She watches the sky change, the moon covered by swirling clouds. She waits to go back until the sky is black and the fires among the wagons die to embers. From the woods, she walks slowly, her arms stretched out in front for protection, but she still trips on an unseen tree root. As she approaches the circus tents and wagons, the light is better, and she moves without stumbling. The sounds of the circus are muted, and she hears only the snorts of sleep and the restless pacing of animals in their cages. She opens the door and enters the dwarves' wagon. From the way they breathe, she knows they only pretend to be asleep. In the frail light coming through the open door, she sees the twisted blankets near the door where Rudy sleeps. He is not there. His satchel is gone. The nail where Terry the Terrier's leash hangs is empty. She feels the urgency in the way every dwarf is holding his or her breath, trying to be silent. She closes the door and gropes her way to her spot on the floor. When she lies on her pallet and closes her eyes, she hears a train whistle, a discharge of steam, and the stutter of steel wheels on iron rails, and she does not know if it is real or imagined.

She sits up. "Where is Rudy?"

"He's gone. We don't know," someone says.

"We can get someone to fill in for the act," whispers another.

"It's not the act," Didi cries, surprised at her anger. She lies back down, facing the bleak silence of harried dwarves, and the dark. Her shoulder throbs, and the pain seems to march into her chest, toward her heart.

REDDOG

On Christmas Day my second year in prison for murder, my mother stopped coming to visit. She doesn't call and I can't get in touch with her. In August, she missed my twenty-fifth birthday. A couple months later, my sister came and said, "Mother doesn't want to think about it anymore. Try to understand." I did try.

Eventually my sister quit coming; she had a lot on her mind with her van full of kids – and no husband. So I go a year with no visitors, and when I get dragged to administration to face an assistant to the warden, I'm half-crazy.

"A graduate student working in criminal justice wants to include you in her experiments," he said. "Your choice. Two or three times a month. Goes on your record as good behavior."

Sessions would be out of maximum security . . . like a mini-vacation.

"Hey. What's with the experiments," I said. "She stick you with drugs, stuff like that?"

"Just talk."

"Hey, Captain. She a looker?"

"Don't get your fantasies revved up. She's a pro."

"You be there?"

"Just you and her. And high security."

"Maybe I get out of max sooner?" I asked. You get a cell in the main building and you could talk to guys, set things up.

"Can't promise." He walked around the table, stuck a ballpoint pen in my cuffed hand, and showed me where to sign. "Consent papers."

You need a magnifying glass to read the print on the last two pages. "I don't know about signing anything," I said.

"It's permission to talk, record, use information," he said.

"I thought this was research," I said. I hated do-gooders and I didn't need rehabilitation. I needed parole, miraculous DNA evidence, a new trial.

"I don't give a shit what you do. I'm here because the warden says to cover our ass legally. It's routine. No one's trying to screw you. No one cares."

"She ain't a lawyer, is she? She ain't trying to retry the case or something."

"She's a student. We checked. She was a paralegal before she went back to grad school. She's demonstrated against the death penalty. Arrested once, but never charged. She won't violate your rights, if that's what you're thinking. You don't have rights."

I signed her papers with a bump-and-a-line so no one could ever read my name.

The researcher, a Ms. Pearlstein, shows up the next day for our first session; she wants to see how things might go. I'm cool, out of maximum security in the south extension, but still with two guards, one inside and one outside the door, and me chained hand and foot.

She was maybe five feet two, wore these thick glasses made the dark of her eyes look like raisins, and her voice had this whine like an echo of metal cut with a circular saw. She was sitting on a folding chair with her skinny legs crossed, her head tilted down. She asked me a few questions, like how I felt about prison, and if I was guilty. I told her prison was like heaven and I wasn't guilty.

"What you studying?" I asked.

She wanted to talk about *the* crime and *my* punishment. What did I care? I was feeling like an eagle soaring. And I'd tell her anything to keep this going, get out of max.

"Accidents happen," I said.

"It was no accident," she said.

"You're good looking," I said, smiling.

She didn't smile back. "I'm not here to talk about me," she said.

"You got a boy friend?"

She sighed. "I have essential questions to ask."

"You the boss, babe."

She frowned, then glared at me like she could see in my brain. "I want to know everything that happened that day. How you felt. What you were thinking," she said.

"It's in the trial stuff, baby."

"You may call me Ms. Pearlstein. I know the trial transcripts well. Trials deal with evasions of the truth." She still gave me her hard look.

I waited. Then I said, "Hey, little lady. You think I lied? That what's scratching your ass?"

"I am not the 'little lady'."

I laughed. "You Ms. Pearlstein," I said.

"I don't know if you lied. I want to know what you and Hershel Cracken were thinking, moment by moment."

"Talk to Reddog. He's the guy give you the story."

Everyone called Hershel Cracken "Reddog," and he was waiting on a lethal at Huntsville; I was in this place for life.

"I've been talking to Hershel, too," Ms. Pearlstein said.

"He ain't called Hershel!"

"How do you feel about him?"

"We're buddies," I said.

"No! His execution."

"Hey. You reap just what you sow."

She glared again. "Are you religious?"

She was writing again, and I was staring at her when a thought came to me like being run over by an eighteen-wheeler.

"You working for the 'Dog? Appeal stuff? That what you here for?"

"I am not working for Hershel. I work for justice. And I will try to find out any detail that might help in an appeal. Something that might contradict testimony and raise a reasonable doubt."

"That ain't research," I said.

"It is very much a part of my research. It's about criminal justice." She looked in her stack of papers and pulled out a sheet. "What you say is used for science. How prisoners think. I'll analyze our sessions for response quality." She talked loudly and slowly, as if I didn't speak English. "Part of our work is truth in meaning. Our sessions are analyzed by independent graders. You can see it in this representation." She adjusted the sheet of paper with colored bars on it so I could see better. "The red bars represent silence, green bars are for meaningful talk, and black bars, for diversions from the truth. Everyone's graph is different. My work relates responses to personalities and various crimes. I specialize in murder."

That was real rat shit. And that's what I told her. I raised my hand to her, my chains rattling.

"Sean brought it on himself," I said. "We didn't do nothing."

"I don't believe that, at all," she said. "Sean was murdered. It's clear from the transcripts, from the autopsy, and the witnesses, before and after."

I looked right at her. "You do guys?" I asked.

She jerked back like I might have slapped her.

"Let's review the rules," she said coldly, "I'm a professional. I won't respond to personal questions."

"Hey. You my woman," I said. She must have done guys; if she were a dyke, she'd probably need to come out with it. But she was shaking, not looking at me. She was deciding whether to pack up her stuff. Her shoulders slumped.

"Can't you be human?" she said.

"I'm swelled up human for you, baby," I said, looking to see if she got my meaning.

"Just answer the questions!" Then, from her folder, she took out a loose sheet of paper with lines and boxes on it, and she put it down on the table.

"What are you in for?" she asked.

"B and E."

"Your record says murder two."

"People get confused. Screw up the truth," I laughed.

"It's a lie. An outright lie."

"Why ask?"

She paused. "It's routine. Demographics. I want to hear it from you."

"I stole a bicycle," I said.

She stood up. She wasn't higher than my armpit if I'd been standing unchained.

"I expected you to cooperate!" she said. "You're nothing but lies."

"You only been here twenty minutes," I said, but she was hurrying to get out. "You coming back?"

"Why should I?" she said over her shoulder.

"You the chief," I said. "Me the Indian."

She had her stuff together and she turned to me. Her face was red. "You are one miserable human being. If I come back, I expect you to treat me with respect. I am an educated woman and a researcher. You are a murderer. I don't want you talking down to me again."

"I ain't no murderer," I said.

Back in my cell, I had this anger, like I wanted to put my fist through the wall. I did fifty push-ups and a hundred squats. Then I was sitting on the bed laughing, thinking to myself, and I figured I'd put her crooked little face right up there on the wall, head high, where I could see her while standing over the toilet for a piss. I had a marking pen. I drew pictures on the wall I copied from magazines – of airplanes, tattoos I'd like, guns, motorcycles, cars. So I draw her face with a small circle about half the real size of her. I point the chin a little. Her nose is almost nothing, so I put two dots for her nose holes. Then I scratch in hair that looks almost like a wig, step back, and laugh at how close I have come to the real Pearlstein. Then I draw in circles and curves for her eyes – close together, looking off to one side like she did most of the time in the session – and after two eyebrow arches, I put thick glasses on. For her mouth, I use a thin line, mean looking. She looked fragile next to my big drawing of a Harley Fatboy, copied straight out of *Motorcycle Cruiser,* like a child who wasn't telling it like it was.

As it turned out, my next session with Pearlstein was only two days later; she looked different, less dry and peely than I remembered, more like some guy's ugly baby sister. I guessed she was twenty-five, but her hair looked a lot older, gray like cobwebs and tight old-lady curls. At least she'd combed her hair, so it didn't look as if she were in a tornado.

Her picture was still on my wall and it didn't need changing; I had her eyes right – close together and small, like she was peeking out of her skull through half-inch drill holes. I'd been laughing at my picture. Cocky little bitch. I wasn't angry no more, but I was surprised she showed up, like she was hot for our sessions more than she let on.

The guards always chained me to the same iron ring sunk in one of the concrete floor blocks, but she was farther away from me today. She must of asked for the new spot – the guards didn't give a damn about where she sat as long as I couldn't reach her. The dented metal table between us was about as long as she was tall, with its legs bolted to the floor. She was looking at her papers, so I rattled my chains. The inside guard looked over at me. I was feeling good, so good. Here in all this space, and there was sunlight coming between the iron bars in the window that laid out long boxes of yellowed light on the gray-white linoleum floor. Sweet, sweet! Ain't no sunshine in maximum.

She wrote on her pad for a while.

"You a real doc?" I asked her.

"Does it make a difference?" She still stared at her pad. Her voice was a little squeaky.

"You ain't one, or you would have said so."

She shifted in her chair. "Please try to keep to the subject."

"You my subject, sweetie pie."

"Ms. Pearlstein," she said angrily.

"You got a first name. Like Virginity?"

"Where were you when you first saw Sean McGarity?"

"Maybe you called Chastity. Chastity Pearlstein!"

"Answer my question."

"I love the way your lips wiggle," I said.

She slammed her folder on the table. "I don't like smartasses," she said. "I've got too much to do." She nodded to the guard and she picked up her papers and her tape recorder. She'd spent less than five minutes with me. That was no session!

"Up yours," I said, but she was already out the door. The guard pointed at me, his first finger straight out like the barrel of a gun. The bastard. The guard closed the door and called for transfer. In a few seconds, I'd be on my way back to maximum.

The room got silent except for the A/C fan. I rested my chained hands on the table. There was a tap on the door. Soft, like a woman. The inside guard turned the key in the lock, and Pearlstein came back in and stared at me as if I was dog shit on her shoe. She whispered to the guard, her jaw clenched. She came back to the table.

"I'll forget your antics," she said.

"Why you pissed?" I asked.

She paused. "I care too much about what I do sometimes."

"Lighten up," I said.

"I *don't* need *your* advice. When did you first see Sean?"

I kept my mouth shut.

Her lips were in a hard line. "Are you refusing to talk?" she asked. "Why can't you answer simple questions?"

"You think I'm going to change my story. Well, I ain't changing my story."

"Damn it. I want to find out what the real story is . . . the story beneath what's been told."

"Reddog's guilty. I ain't guilty," I said. "That's the truth."

"You were both convicted."

"He got what was coming."

"He got murder one because you plea bargained."

"That ain't research talk," I said.

"You have given me so many black bars for my research. You can't tell the truth about anything!"

We sat in silence while she stared at her notes.

"I'll tell you the truth. You my honey."

"I am not your honey!"

She uncrossed her legs and put both feet solid on the floor.

"You'll never get Reddog off," I said.

"Think what you want," she said. She was straightening her papers by holding the edges and tapping the stack-bottom on the table. Her index finger twitched.

"You can't blow his conviction," I said.

"How could you possibly know?"

"You can ask more questions."

"I'm wasting my time."

"For Reddog, or research?" I asked, but she didn't answer. Her mind was locked on Reddog like a fly on cow shit. The research gig might be legit, but it wasn't what she'd give her virginity for. She wanted the 'Dog alive. The guard unlocked the door for her, sliding the dead bolt. She walked out. Within minutes the transfer guys were taking me back to max.

In my cell, I took my marking pen and changed my drawing of her head. I added a stick drawing of her body with arms and legs, and then I put a line between where her thighs might be, a line like a stick jammed up her twat. It was crude, but I felt better.

※

Each day, I wondered if I would get out for a session. Security guys had scrotal squeeze about advanced notice giving cons the edge for escape attempts. For guys in max with no outside contacts, it didn't seem to make no difference.

After five days, I was moved back to the session room about two hours before lunch. Pearlstein sat straight in her chair with both feet on the floor. She looked more like a girl now; I mean she had her little tits poking up under a red sweater. Her glasses were bent, sitting a little crooked on her face, and she kept taking hold of the corner of the frame and sliding them up her nose.

She started right in with questions.

"I see your mother hasn't been coming to visit."

"Aren't you the little detective," I said.

"You don't care about your mother?" she asked.

"She's a fat slob. I didn't choose her. No one would have chosen her."

"What's she do?"

"She goes out of the house once a month to pick up her welfare and ADC checks."

Pearlstein did a lot of busy writing.

"You ain't making bars," I said.

"My associates do the graphs on a computer at school."

"Well, my mother ain't worth a shit. Put that on a graph."

"Did you feel that way when she was still visiting?"

"She wasn't no good then, either."

She waited before she spoke again. When she looked up, she had wrinkles on her brow and she squinted at me.

"Hey. You giving conjugals to the 'Dog?'" I asked.

"You're crude."

"But I ain't stupid," I said. "The research is like a decoy in a bank robbery."

"I never said you were stupid," she said, swallowing hard.

"But that's what you think!" My heart pounded and I strained at my wrist-cuffs.

"You'll never know what I'm thinking. Never in a thousand years."

"I don't have to take shit from no student trainee," I said. "You ain't even a real doc!"

She shoved her chair back and looked up. "Okay," she said. "Calm down. It was not the right thing to say." She went back to her pad, writing fast. I tried making my mind blank, squeezing her out. It was a prison thing to do, to be sure nothing ever got to you. But I was still breathing hard and fast. I stared at her, the way she was hunched over, her hair over her ears hiding most of her face. Her pencil stuck up between her first finger and her bird-finger, and it made these little circles as she wrote. I hadn't seen anything like that since grade school. There was a lot about Ms. Pearlstein that came out slow, and only if you looked hard.

After a few minutes, she began picking up her stuff but stayed seated. "Think about it Billie," she said. "Talking about it doesn't make any difference now. There will never be a retrial for you. But you could save a man from dying."

"You ain't leaving?" I said.

"I want justice, Billie. It's so easy." She looked small but solid. She wasn't backing down on anything.

"I understand what you're saying," I said.

"Do you, Billie? Do you know what justice is? The difference between right and wrong?"

"I been to school."

"It's more than that, Billie. It's what's inside."

"What you really needing, baby?"

"You were driving the truck when Sean went down. I know that. The world knows that. But if you said it, we might have an appeal."

"The kid asked for it," I said.

"You know what the world believes? It was gay bashing. You'll never change that. But you could keep a man alive."

"Reddog tied the kid to the truck. He hugged the kid to make him feel good." She looked more interested than I had ever seen. "He grabbed the kid's crotch and stroked him, until the kid laughed and said 'That's all me.'"

"But you were driving!"

I shut up.

"Think about it Billie. The truth won't hurt you now."

"Sean wasn't my kind of guy," I said. He'd been out of the closet since the day he was born. He wore tan slacks with that slick-soft cloth that never wrinkles, and a white girly shirt unbuttoned at the top so the no-hair skin on his chest showed halfway down to his belly button. He ran his fingers through his hair to keep it sticking up for that I-just-got-out-of-bed look. He stroked this little, light mustache, with hairs that looked like he stole them from a caterpillar and pasted them on one by one. The kid drank screwdrivers!

"But you were the one who accelerated the truck to more than sixty miles an hour, dragging the helpless boy until his clothes and skin were gone, his face smashed! Say it!"

"Reddog's guilty."

"You were driving!"

"Fuck off."

She held her breath, her hands clenched in bloodless fists. She turned slowly, all of her belongings cradled in her arms.

"You coming back?" I called to her.

Alone in my cell with my black marker, I covered her body with a dress so that line in her twat was blotted out. She looked better with a dress on. And I hadn't been feeling good about hurting her with a stick like that. But I drew shackles around each foot, with chains hanging down, every link showing as if it might drag her off the wall.

∽∞∽

It was three days later when Pearlstein came back, two hours earlier than she ever did before, just after breakfast. I'd cooled down a bit, and I'd been thinking about our last session. She was doing what she had to do. I was determined not to take it to heart. Especially the truth part; she didn't tell the whole truth neither.

She was already in the room when the guards brought me in.

"Hi," I said.

She didn't say anything, just sat, her chair pushed back from the table. Her skinny legs were crossed and her knobby kneecap stuck up like a baby turtle shell on a log when you're out shooting squirrels. She doodled on her pad.

"You want to talk?" she finally asked.

"Don't make no difference to me," I said. I stared. Her dress was green, the shade of summer grass, and it made her hair look the color of rain clouds. Her skin was as white as a shower-stall wall, and she had a few pimple-crater scars on her cheeks. One was still reddish and big enough to hurt when she touched it. She had holes in her ears for earrings. I wondered what Pearlstein wore on the outside. Studs? Those long dangling earrings that might shimmy when she moved her head? Pussy counselors took off their jewelry for sessions, so I'd never know what she wore.

"It really wasn't me," I finally said. "If that's what you want to know."

"Even your mother doesn't believe that." She crossed her legs and pulled her dress down, covering her knee.

"What did my mother say?"

"She said you worshiped Reddog. Couldn't sit still when he was away. That you were a good boy until you met him."

"We were just buddies."

"Reddog said you were the one."

"Look," I said. "Reddog set the kid up! I didn't set the kid up!"

"Why did you do that?"

I thought out what she wanted to hear. "We didn't find no babes in Jolly's bar, but Sean comes in, light on his feet, looking for guys. The 'Dog thought he'd have some laughs."

"So Reddog approached Sean?"

I was about to say the kid was grinning at Reddog and he waved the kid over to him, but before I could get the words out, Pearlstein called the guard over from where he stood near the door. Her skin was even paler now than usual, and sweat glinted on her brow.

"You want to hear about it?" I asked. But Ms. Pearlstein stood up. She had to go to the bathroom. God, how I wished I had a cigarette... but tobacco was banned.

She was gone a long time before she came back and sat down, and I waited, thinking she'd ask a question. Nothing. Like she'd forgotten what we were talking about. The time was ticking on, the hour getting shorter.

"I'm not feeling good," she said.

"You look like a ghost," I said.

"It's probably some flu."

She shut off the recorder and put a rubber band around her rolled up sheets of scribbles. She wasn't allowed to bring a brief case into secure rooms.

"Don't go," I said.

"Maybe tomorrow."

It was funny, but I hoped she felt better.

"A glass of water," I said to guard. He didn't move.

"She's sick," I said. "Grab her some water?"

He signaled to the outside guard who brought water in a paper cup.

"She's wasting her time with you," the inside guard said, soft and mean, to me.

She drank the water, looking down. Within minutes, she was back looking at me.

"You better?" I asked.

She didn't answer. She turned on the recorder. She shuffled some papers and looked at the electric clock on the wall.

"I can't understand why Sean went with you," Pearlstein said in a raspy voice, like she might have been vomiting.

"You really okay?"

"I'm better. I thought you were the sweet talking guy," she said. "Reddog was the strong silent type."

"You got that right," I said with pride.

"But it was Reddog, then, that talked Sean into going with you?"

"That's right."

Reddog might not have been a big talker, but he had a molasses-sweet voice that turned heads. And he was the best looking man in five states. People took to him, remembered him like a good chunk of hot pecan pie with ice cream. And this kid Sean fell for Reddog after one look.

"He was in love with the 'Dog. Couldn't keep his eyes off him."

I waited. For the first time, she wasn't doodling or squiggling. Her right hand was pressed flat on her stomach.

"Reddog drove when you left the bar?" she asked.

"The kid in the middle between me and the 'Dog." I remembered the kid's knee was shoved against my thigh because of the gearshift on the floor, but the kid's hand was on the 'Dog's thigh.

"'Cool wheels,' the kid said.

"'Where you get shitty talk like that,' Reddog said. 'Cool wheels? You queer or something?' Then the kid laughed."

"How did you get Sean behind the truck?"

"Reddog smooth talking," I said. "Reddog made it sound like weight training, you had to push yourself to get better, keep tight and fit."

Pearlstein raised her pencil to me, holding it like a cop's nightstick. "When Sean got behind the truck, didn't you drive Reddog's truck?"

"You keep asking that. This ain't cross examination."

"I can understand it started out as a game. But it wasn't a game when the driver jammed that accelerator to the floor."

The kid was exactly what Reddog said he hated: wimpy look, whiney voice, sissy shoes, pale lips, pukey mustache. But Reddog enjoyed setting the kid up for showing him what a queer he was. And he liked touching him. Teasing him.

"How did Sean fall down?"

Pearlstein's tape had stopped spinning. It needed a turning but I said nothing. Pearlstein was quiet, the smooth top of her ballpoint pen clenched between her teeth.

"I think you were jealous, Billie."

I laughed. "Of Sean? You got your head up your ass."

"Did you try to save Sean?"

"Sure," I said thinking hard. "I did everything." I looked right at Pearlstein. "He was gasping. His right eye was puffy and almost shut; the other eyelid was half-open, his eyeball rolled up so it showed only white. I pushed on the kid's chest, CPR stuff from the Army. Blood all over me."

"I never heard this. Did Reddog do anything?" Pearlstein asked.

"Nothing!"

"Who said bury him," Pearlstein asked.

"'We've got to get rid of him,' Reddog said."

"Not you?"

"Not me!"

I looked at Pearlstein to see if she believed me, but she had her eyes down looking at her paper. Her pencil wiggled a little, then went still.

"You know about Reddog's trial?" she asked.

"I heard." We were caught before the kid settled in his grave. Four people saw us leave Jolly's.

"It took the jury two hours to convict him," she said.

The cops hated Reddog, and they wanted the world to think the Texas justice system was lubed to smooth-running with I'll-fix-your-ass grease. The prosecutors ate up my plea bargain.

"You think the jury was wrong about Reddog?" Pearlstein asked.

"They got off on giving him the max," I said.

Her eyelids drooped. Her pen was still now.

"What story he tell you?" I asked.

Pearlstein looked at me. "Not that."

"Would I lie to you?"

"You weren't driving when Sean went down?"

"What'd I tell you?" I said. I must have shouted or something close to it, because she squinted. And the truth was, I was driving when Sean went down. Reddog was leaning his head out the window, calling to the little fucker from the passenger side, telling him he was doing great. The little shit. I shoved the accelerator, the engine straining to do the hundred and twenty it had done for me plenty of times.

"You think I'd lie?" I asked.

She shuffled her papers into a pile. I was strangely calm.

"You're the one who should be waiting for execution," she said.

Pearlstein gathered up her tape recorder and paper stack without a word.

"Time's not up," I said. The way she was grabbing things up looked like she wasn't thinking about coming back.

She didn't look to me.

"Okay . . . I was driving . . . but it didn't make any difference. Reddog *was* guilty." She was looking around, and then she found her pencil.

"He tied the knot. Put the kid behind the truck," I said.

Anger blazed in her eyes. I thought she was going to spit at me.

"I was driving when the kid went down! You can tell them that."

She was writing on the outside of a folder without putting her stuff down. "And you sped up. Faster than any human could run."

"Yeah. You can tell them that too."

She was breathing hard.

"What more do you want?" I asked.

"I don't know," she said. "The Governor has refused a stay. But I'll try. It may be too late."

"You coming back?"

She reached the door. She turned her steady gaze to me. In the shadows, her eyes were the size of bore holes in a pistol.

Back in my cell, the evil hard lines of her drawing bugged me. I wet a few squares of toilet paper and tried to wash her off the wall, but the swipes just blurred the lines, and the terrible shape of her still would not fade. I took off the two inch metal handle from the toilet flusher, and I hacked at the wall, at the drawing, crumbling the painted cement block inch by inch until she was gone, just a pile of crumbled wall-dust at my feet.

I sat on my bunk. I looked at the pile of dust and trash as if she were still there. I could never draw her again, and for a crazy moment I wondered if I could put her back together – glue, or tape, or something. But she was destroyed. Hell, it was just a drawing. And I had every right to be pissed at her. She was the one who'd lied to me about experiments. All that talk about truth. Truth don't mean nothing!

I had to sweep out the cell at clean-up the next morning. Damn if the guard didn't deny workout sessions in the exercise yard for a week for destroying the wall. Christ, it was only the top part of the concrete, not a hole or anything.

The 'Dog was put down with appeal denied. Word spread through the prison, even in maximum security, as if there were no walls. And I waited, thinking maybe the research might start up again. But the days went by for more than three months. The patch of destroyed wall never changed until some maintenance guy slapped some plaster on it when I was getting eye care in the infirmary. Pearlstein didn't show, and the lost picture I'd drawn on the wall stayed with me only in mind, trapped in its own cell.

A few weeks later, my mind started playing tricks on me. It happens to cons. One night, I heard the 'Dog. He was behind a closed door at the end of the hall. His voice was soft, and I couldn't make out the words. Then it was gone. Days later, in the middle of the night, the lights on low illumination, I heard him taking a piss. I knew I couldn't see him, and I didn't try. The next night, he came standing in the shadows, just outside the bars, maybe five feet back near the opposite wall. Just an outline, but I knew he was wearing a tank top, tight jeans. I knew, too, the shape of his lats, the curve of his delts and biceps. He stood there, motionless, silent, and then he was gone before I could think to call out to him.

CAPTAIN WITHERS'S WIFE

In 1963, on an American base in France, Amy Withers loaded her husband's hair-trigger automatic pistol, called the military police, wrapped her newborn baby in a hand-knitted beige afghan with a purple border, and waited at the front window of her commonplace bungalow. The policeman arrived, parked his car near the curb, and walked toward the house. She opened the front window from above and shot four rounds into the air.

The policeman backed away. "We got a call . . ."

"I called," Amy yelled. "I want the commander."

The policeman swore. "You need a shrink," he mumbled.

"I heard that, you creep." She shot another round into the air.

Amy grabbed the baby, left the afghan on the floor. She opened the door and shoved the baby out, grabbing his clothing over his spine and supporting his bottom with the right hand still holding the gun.

"I'm afraid I'll hurt him."

"I'm not calling the commander!" He crouched behind the car, his gun drawn.

Amy closed the door and went to the window. Her next bullet made a hole in the rear door window of the police car.

The policeman crawled into the front seat from the passenger side, keeping his head down. He called for backup. A second car arrived with a superior officer. From a safe distance and with a bullhorn, the new officer demanded Amy's surrender. When Amy didn't respond, he zigzagged toward the front door of the house with a weapon under his flack vest. Crouching, he knocked.

The door opened six inches and the automatic came out. He couldn't see the woman.

"Give me the baby," he said standing up.

"I want the commander."

"The commander can't come."

"Captain Withers has left me without a dime."

The superior officer grabbed for the gun. Amy lurched back and shot above his head. He flattened against the wall at the side of the door and reached for his pistol. Amy came out, the baby cradled in her arm, and pointed the automatic at the superior officer's left eye. He removed his hand from the vest and showed her his palm.

"Look," said Amy pushing the child forward so he could see without moving. "You know my husband. Blond. Blue eyed. Does this look like my husband?"

The kid was really small. The eyes were darker than any he could ever remember in a baby. And the thin hair swept on top of the pink scalp like a wave breaking on the shore was black, not blond.

"It's on your conscience . . . anything happens," Amy pressed.

The officer relaxed a little. "Mothers can't kill their children."

"Just call the commander. Use my name. He knows me."

She slammed the door shut with her foot and went back to wait in front of her window where she could watch all the activity on the street. The baby cried when she wrapped him in the afghan a put him on the floor.

"Hush," she said. "You got me into this mess."

She reloaded.

By the time the superior officer returned to his command center, he had decided to contact the commander. He did not like the commander, who was only a full colonel temporarily appointed as commander until a general could be found. The superior officer half-smiled at the opportunity to annoy the commander with leadership trivia. The call went out from base communications, and within thirty minutes the commander – who was divorced and liked to party – was found in a private room at the officer's club.

"We got a dependent with a gun threatening to kill her baby," the senior officer said over a static filled line.

"Take her in. You can't let it get out of control," the commander barked.

"It's Amy Withers. That's what she said to tell you."

The pause at the commander's end of the line was brief but definitive. "She's crazy. Call the doc. Send her to the loony bin."

"I should wait for the doc? Do nothing?"

"You deaf?" The commander rang off.

The superior officer smirked to himself.

When the call about Amy came, the doctor – in his bungalow of the type specially assigned to high-ranking officers of major and above – was sitting on the edge of a bed massaging his wife's nude back. She was face down, the bottom part of her body under a sheet, her bent arms splayed out on each side of the pillow supporting her shaved head, flawlessly done daily by her best girlfriend, whose head she shaved in return.

"Don't answer it," his wife said in habitual, cold, detached words that he had learned to ignore over the last ten years of marriage. At least when they had been stationed in Minnesota, she had enjoyed horseback riding and private yoga instruction. But now she rarely ventured beyond the perimeter fence that surrounded the base, reluctantly playing bridge in the cramped living rooms of older women who dealt cards with a flask of gin cradled on the floor between their ankles.

"I'm on call, J.D.," he said reaching for the phone. She slapped his arm and he paused. The phone rang again.

"You didn't tell me you were on call." She believed the twice-weekly massage he gave her for back pain would, if divided into parts, lose its therapeutic continuity. "Don't go."

The phone rang again.

"I hate this place," she said, but he heard "I hate you." Maybe he hadn't been around enough early in their marriage, or maybe he should have left her with her mother in Florida when he was assigned overseas, but was he really to blame? After internship she insisted he go into general practice in the military when he had been accepted for a residency in psychiatry. For years, her headaches – and sudden bouts of fatigue in moments of affection – had all but extinguished his desire for her. And last month she vacationed with her friend at Mont Blanc, and without him.

When he answered the phone she stood up with her back to him, covering herself with a towel, and went to the bathroom to dress.

The doctor climbed into the commander's limousine parked a safe distance from the front of Amy Withers's house. The commander was a lanky swarthy man with a high voice, whose appearance on the scene of domestic unrest was unusual and puzzling.

"She's crazy, doc. You need to give her a tranquillizer or something. Commit her so we can fly her back emergency," the commander said as the doctor closed the door.

"Who is it?" the doctor asked. The base was small. Everyone knew everyone.

"Withers's wife."

The doctor's heart beat hard and fast. Amy Withers. Just her name made him feel her presence. She had strong efficient limbs and a face of natural beauty, a smell of freshness, and a hushed way of speaking.

More than a year ago she had walked into his office. She was distraught. Her husband played around. She blamed herself for failing to recreate her mother and father's almost perfect marriage. To help her cope, the doctor increased her appointments to twice a week; soon, he knew everything about her, and she began to stop talking in mid-sentence and stare out a window, her eyes moist from lost dreams and her body rigid with longing for an omen of hope. The silences were so intense he was, in the beginning, afraid to intrude; but when he sensed her need and finally asked his softly worded questions about what she believed, what she wanted in life, what her dreams told her, he was captivated by her openness. She was unable to lie about her world or herself, even by omission. One time she stared and he did not look away, their eyes filled only with each other, and he could only recover his composure by thumbing through his appointment calendar for no reason, his heart quickened with joy and dread.

Toward the end, she came as often as every other day. Even though anticipation of her arrival crowded his mind and only the sight of her dampened his longing, he was meticulously professional at every session. He hid his reverence when she was near as best he could and he kept the sessions to exactly thirty minutes, unfailingly mentioning at the end of their time how much progress she had made. Then, without warning, ten minutes into the final session, he was consumed by an urge to compliment her, to tell her how he admired her resilience, how he loved the indescribable blue of her eyes, how he had come to measure the timing of his breathing to the exact intake of her own air. He stood silently to face the window, his back to her.

"Are you sick?" Amy had asked. He terminated the session immediately, making an excuse about an emergency. That afternoon, speaking to the receptionist, he assured that all future treatments for Amy Withers were referred to a colleague.

Amy never spoke to him again. On the few occasions when he would see her in the waiting room, or at the base commissary, she would avoid his gaze. He waved to her once, but she turned away. Soon, she stopped coming to the clinic.

The doctor squirmed on the limousine's leather seat.

The commander straightened his career service ribbons from habit. The doctor was oddly distracted, as if unaware of the severity of the problem. "Look, Doc. You got to talk to her," the commander said.

"Storm the place," the doctor said.

"She's good with the gun. She could have killed the MP."

The doctor desperately sought a solution that would avoid contact.

"You talk to her then," the doctor said.

"I'm through talking to her. She's nuts."

"What's she want?"

"Money! She can fly back on a government plane as a dependent. And she's on standby. But Withers has cut her off. She wants me to garnish his salary to guarantee her income. Make up back pay. She's thought about it. I don't even know if I can garnish a Captain's salary without legal proceedings."

"Do what she wants. Withers is a cheating son-of-a-bitch. "

"I'm working on it. But she says she's afraid she'll kill the kid."

"Her baby?" A baby was news to the doctor and confusion made him avoid the commander's stare.

The commander frowned. "I can't afford a wrong guess on what she might or might not do," he said waving his hand in dismissal. "You got something to knock her out?"

A call came in over the radio and the limousine driver lowered the window separating the front seat from the back. Staff members at headquarters had not found the administrator who could solve garnishment problems, the driver said. Yes, they were hurrying! The commander reached across the doctor for the door handle and shoved him out of the car. "Commit her!"

"You need a plan," the doctor said.

"Goddamn it. You keep her calm. I'll be back in touch."

From the street, the doctor searched the front of the house for signs of Amy. The sun had set but he could see the front window was open a crack . . . he could not see her or a weapon.

On the narrow path, he tried to stride confidently toward the house, stumbling once on a crack in the concrete obscured by the dark. He reminded himself that the woman he remembered would not shoot him. The front door opened. He paused at the threshold. He saw the standard living room of all base housing—a couch next to the wall with a framed picture of an American flag over it. A small lamp glowed on a side table.

"Hello," he called as he stepped up on the stoop. Amy was behind the door, out of the line of fire. Could she hear him? There was growing noise from the vehicles arriving in front of the house and the chatter of neighbors who had been evacuated and huddled near a canvas-backed supply truck that provided coffee and pastries, the engine running, the headlights creating long shadows on the street and sidewalks.

"Mrs. Withers?" The doctor entered cautiously. She closed the door behind them.

"My God. Why would they send you?"

"The commander sent me."

"I don't need a doctor. Especially you!"

"The commander wants you hospitalized. I was on call."

She was not insane. Her dark blue eyes still mirrored a rational determination he had always admired.

"I need money to go home."

"The commander's working on it."

"That bastard."

"We could wait at the hospital," he said.

"So I won't kill my child?"

"Does it have milk?"

She slumped onto the two-seater sofa, the gun on the cushion next to her. He stayed near the closed door. She put her head in her hands – her fingers buried in her golden hair – her elbows on her bare knees, the hem of her wrinkled dress carelessly resting at mid-thigh. She did not cry.

"It's only a baby. But I hate it enough."

He pulled up a straight-backed wooden government-issue chair.

"We've been eating at Mary Wheeler's house," Amy said. "My father died in April and mother's alone on social security. And my husband has cut me off."

"He has to support you."

She leaned back, her hands loosely by her sides, her head extended with her chin up slightly. The front of her dress gaped where a button was lost.

"No one likes your husband. But he can't be so bad that he won't support his child."

She exhaled. "It's not his."

"Oh, Amy. Does he know?"

"Of course he knows."

"Did you tell the commander?"

"I didn't need to tell the commander."

"If he knew, I'm sure he could find some way to get you support."

"What's he going to do? He sent you."

"He's working on it. He wants me to calm you."

"He wants to get rid of me."

The doctor felt sympathy at first, then betrayal. How often he had thought of her since her therapeutic sessions, always in an aura of her dedicated longing for him. He assumed an unstated lifetime of dedication to each other that those silent sessions had implied.

"How could you?" the doctor said.

"Don't judge me," Amy retorted, "I was alone on a week-long religious retreat. I needed someone. The commander said he loved me. I was a fool to believe him."

She sat up straight, both feet on the floor, a space between her back and the sofa so that her hair cascaded behind her when she used both hands to gather it off her shoulders.

"I'm sure the commander will do something," he said leaning forward, his forearms on his thighs, his eyes fixed on the reflection of the lamp on his black patent leather shoes.

"I've tried for weeks. He won't even see me."

"Well, he was working on it when I came in."

"And he wants to commit me!"

The doctor had his hands together, his fingers interlocked. His knuckles had turned white. "I'll wait with you," he said.

She leaned back again. The gun slipped from the cushion to the floor discharging a muffled shot into the wall behind the sofa toward the kitchen. She brought it closer to her carelessly with her foot and picked it up. "Don't even think about trying to make a move. I'm a good shot."

He had not thought about it. He was not a hero.

"You're partly to blame," she said. "Those sessions."

The shot had unnerved him; his mouth was dry. He looked to the baby on the floor near the window. It dozed, spit dribbling down the side of its face.

"Weren't they helpful?" he asked hoarsely.

She didn't speak, turning her gaze to him. He looked away.

"You cared," she said softly.

"I was glad to help," he answered.

"No. You wanted me. I needed that."

He had longed for her over these many months, and he had fought against his need to act, to risk contacting her, to tell her why he terminated that last session.

"I won't shoot the child," she said. "I could never do that."

"You're not a murderer," he said.

"I'm afraid," she said. "No love makes the innocent dry up and blow away . . . it's like murder . . . in a way."

The baby cried and fell silent again.

"Should we take a look?" he asked.

"He's all right!" she said. The baby did turn quiet, lying unaware, and with a trace of a contented smile.

"We can work this out safely in the hospital."

"With me sedated so I won't know who I am?" she said. Screw him and his plans to restrain her. He was a repulsive icon for unstated promises never kept, implied expectations never fulfilled. Could he ever seize a moment? No! She hated him for that.

"I'm not leaving until I get support," she said. The tension in her legs caused her knees to flutter.

She shifted her automatic from one hand to the other. The doctor stayed seated on the chair, his mind a jumble of memories and emotions. He was again obsessed by her presence, aware how alert she made him feel even when she was consumed by anger.

The doctor walked to the window. The silence now in the room, intensified by the sound of the bustle outside, held fear and uncertainty, so different from their therapeutic sessions that had pulsed with longing and potential. The difference hurt.

Amy and the doctor waited in the dim lighting of the living room and didn't speak for a while. Then the doctor went to the bathroom. Amy changed the baby's diaper. Then they sat again, he in his chair, she lying on her sofa, her legs up, the automatic on her breasts rising and falling with her breathing.

"It can't be long now," he said.

He forced himself into his professional mode. He would not try to disarm her. It would only result in disaster. He hoped to rationalize with her – without threats and violence – for a stay in the hospital to resolve her fears, and to satisfy the commander.

"You're not what you pretend," he said. "Life has pushed you to the limits."

She said nothing.

"All those hours together. I know who you are, what you suffered. Don't destroy what you can be."

Her eyes were closed but she was wide-awake.

"It's being here in a foreign country. No support. No one to turn to," he said. "You held on more than most of us could." He knew things could only get worse for Amy, but he tried to remain upbeat.

The baby whimpered again but only for a few seconds. The doctor's stomach growled and he could feel the beat of his heart.

"I loved you," he said. He looked away, surprised at the sound of his own words. He wanted to bring her to the pain of his reality.

She sat straight up with her feet on the floor, the gun resting in the valley made by her dress between her legs.

"You never loved me," she said. "You teased me. You sucked me into fantasies I could never have imagined on my own!"

"No!" he said. "I cared."

"Your wife fills you with hate."

"I was always thinking of you."

"Everyone knows you hate her. You have a void, doctor, a deep void, and I was something that made you know you were still alive. That is not love!"

"I'm a professional, Amy. I was helping."

"Those long silences. That wasn't being a doctor. And it wasn't just to help me!"

He couldn't look at her.

"Look at me. Tell me how you love me, now. That you'll take me away. Make everything all right."

He had loved her. "I'll take you to the hospital," he said. "I promise you I will make it all right."

"Liar. You won't take me . . . support me."

"It was love. I didn't do it to fill a void."

"Where were you all those months? Even now you're here because you were on call. If you love me, say it. Say it with meaning!"

He hesitated. "I love you," he said, but he was afraid of her, unsure of what she, and he, had become.

"Liar!" she said again.

"What more can I do?" Even to himself, he seemed to be pleading.

"Be honest. You lech."

He walked to the window. There were even more vehicles now.

"Get out," she said. "You will never accept me. Married or divorced. Child or childless. It was enough for you to sit there and enjoy the potential. You're sick."

"I'll wait until the commander comes back. I'll help you negotiate."

"I'll always be Amy Withers. Vulnerable patient."

"You need support. That's only fair," he said.

"I've waited too long."

"I'll help, Amy. Let me help," he said. He tried to smile and when she didn't respond he returned to his chair.

"Don't go out of your way," she said. And she positioned herself on the sofa so it was obvious she was through talking.

To his staff, the commander said he was tired of dealing with a pilot's hysterical wife and he couldn't see placing himself, a Base Commander, in a position of danger, no matter how low-risk the danger might be. In truth he could not face Amy's career-smashing truths and accusing glare. He sent his adjutant, a tall, deep-spoken man whom he found industrious, if not overly intelligent. The adjutant calmly knocked on the door.

Amy jumped up from the couch and opened the door cautiously, making sure the commander was alone. It was not the commander, but she let the adjutant in, closing the door and backing away. The adjutant did not salute when the doctor stood. Amy waved with her pistol when the adjutant tried to move; he stopped. The three of them stood in a lopsided triangle facing each other.

"Where's the commander?" Amy asked.

"I'm fully empowered to deal."

"You've brought the papers? Cash?'

"Yes. I've brought papers for application for an exclusive account at the American bank on base. Money can easily be transferred to the states. You sign and I'll take the papers by tomorrow to establish your account for deposit."

"What money?"

"Part of your husband's salary."

"Half of my husband's salary! Guaranteed. Notarized."

"I don't know what percentage they're working on, but fifty per cent sounds reasonable. I'll pass it on."

"And cash to make up for the last six months deposited. I've been cheated."

"The judge advocate is working on a settlement. Your husband has been contacted in Beirut and will be back the day after tomorrow."

"He'll never agree."

"The commander will convince him."

"And no money now?"

"You can live in the hospital. No charge. Maybe the commander can establish a line of credit at the commissary."

The doctor moved closer to the two. "Be straight with her, lieutenant. Don't bullshit."

"Hey. It's only until the legal stuff is worked out. You know the system, Doc. Christ, it's a nightmare."

"She wants what is rightfully hers," the doctor said.

"I know her pain," said the adjutant to the doctor.

"No you don't!" Amy said. "You don't know what it is to be abandoned."

"We all know Withers is not the perfect husband," the adjutant said. Amy moaned.

"This woman has been wronged, Lieutenant."

"We've gone the limit on this one, doc. A lot farther than I think we should have, to tell the truth," the adjutant said.

"You've done nothing," Amy said.

The Adjutant shook his head. She picked up the baby in the afghan, the automatic still in her hand. The adjutant moved toward her. She waved the gun at him. "Stay back." The child cried.

Amy shoved the baby toward him. He made no move to take it.

"You take care of him. You love him. Raise him to be a confident, resourceful human being." She pushed back the afghan from the baby's face so the adjutant could see.

The child certainly didn't look like Withers. He paused looking puzzled.

"Let her go," the doctor said. "Take the baby."

"I plan to," said the adjutant. He reached out with his right palm and pushed the baby and Amy back, and turned to the door to call for help.

The shot rang out as he gripped the doorknob, before he opened the door.

"Oh, God. Dear God," Amy cried.

The Doctor reached out, leaning toward her. The barrel of the gun, discolored now with the infant's gushing blood, waved without purpose at odd angles as Amy struggled to remove her son from the bloody afghan.

"Oh, God," she cried. "He was so innocent."

"You've killed him," the adjutant said.

"*I* didn't kill him," she screamed. "The gun went off." She slumped to the floor on her knees laying the little corpse on the couch, still trying to get the child's legs free from the tangled afghan. The gun barrel jerked toward the doctor and discharged again. A sharp pain pierced the doctor, and his legs gave way. He crumpled to the floor, watching her gaze shift from terror to the wild calmness of despair, then she put the gun to her temple and squeezed the trigger. As she fell forward facedown, her arm draped across the doctor's chest. She took only a few more breaths; he reached out, the flat of his hand on her ribs, and he felt the last beat of her heart. Unable to move his legs, he waited for the adjutant to uncover his eyes. "Get an ambulance," the doctor said.

∞

The doctor allowed his wife to see him in his hospital room three days later. He'd been operated on and had been assured his injuries were not life threatening. But he had needed time to think before talking to her.

She stood by the bedside and took his hand in hers without lifting it off the sheet.

"You're letting your hair grow again," he said. It had some length and had been teased to the stiffness of synthetic carpet.

"My friends don't like it. But I'm glad you noticed."

They suffered a silence without looking at each other.

"It must have been terrible," she said, "Your patient! Everyone says she was crazy from the day she arrived."

He couldn't speak of Amy. She wasn't crazy, even at the end.

"What did you think of her?" she asked.

"She had a lousy marriage. No one would help," he finally managed.

"You liked her?"

He weighed versions of the truth. "I did."

She let go of his hand without moving. "Did you love her?"

He hesitated. "No," he said avoiding her stare.

"There's a rumor she saw you almost every day for weeks at a time."

"She was sick," he said. "She needed help."

"I really don't care if you were screwing her. But I do care if people think you were."

"I wasn't screwing her. It wasn't like that. She was my patient."

His wife rubbed her eye with her knuckle to wipe out some speck of irritation. She sat on the edge of the bed. "Does it hurt? My sitting here?"

"No. I'll never have feeling again. Or movement."

"The doctor told me," she said.

"I'll be in a wheelchair forever. At least with full disability. I was in the line of duty."

"I've made arrangements. We can go to Mother's house. I can have a special room for you on the first floor with wheelchair access."

"We can live close to normal," he said. "I may still be able to have a limited practice."

"You'll do no such thing. You're my disabled husband. We'll do for you. I've ordered bookshelves for your room. A radio/television/stereo combination. And I'll be going back to work. I've already been accepted for a legal-secretary job at a firm I knew well before we were married. With the government check, we'll get along just fine." She was almost exuberant, eager to get on to a new life. She seemed released from some oppressive, crushing restraint.

"All that in just three days?" he asked.

"To tell the truth, I'd been thinking about it for a while. Going back to work. You're being hurt like this just moved it up a year."

"I'm almost surely impotent," he said. "Can you stand an invalid husband?"

"Nonsense talk," she said, moving off the bed. She bent and hugged him, and then kissed him on the forehead.

"I'll be back tomorrow. I've arranged for early return for both of us on med-evac. The movers will pack at the end of the week. I've sold the car for more than it's worth."

She shut the door. He was glad she was gone. When he closed his eyes, Amy Withers was on her couch with her hair pulled back, her blue eyes deep as tiny oceans. He couldn't erase this memory, especially detailed in silent times, and his chest tightened with a dull pain unrelated to his injuries.

His wife returned with a shiny chrome urinal she hung on the side bedrail.

"The nurse asked me," she said. She blew him a kiss as she left. He had never seen her blow kisses – to him, or anyone.

From his bed, looking out the small hospital-room window, he could see only treetops and the French clouds that obscured the blue sky.

THE THIRTEEN NUDES OF ERNEST GOINGS

Amanda Goings parked her station wagon in the unpaved drive to her mother's two story white clapboard house with green trim and a pitched roof that had kept snows from long Maine winters from collecting and crushing the Goings family. The curtains parted on a window to the right of the door. The interior lights were turned off and it was too dark see, but she waved to let her mother know she'd be back in a few minutes to take her to the luncheon. The curtain fell back in place.

She walked fifty yards to the stone wall at the edge of the property, her rubber-soled shoes unsteady on the sheets of wet leaves under the maples and the walnut tree. She came to a ragged break that had been there since her childhood. For thirty-two years, the wall was the divider between the Goings family's property and the neighboring property recently purchased by her father.

She climbed the knoll and passed through a line of cedars. She stumbled near the top, the turned in foot and withered left leg from a birth defect failing to support her adequately. On the downhill slope, invisible from her mother's house and the road, was a barn, the only structure that remained on the property. She swore as she always did when she saw the two rectangular roof skylights that mirrored northern light from grey overhead clouds. She thought the expensive renovation of the barn a waste of money – split levels floored with slate and twelve-inch antique floorboards, directional track lighting, and an open-loft living facility adjacent to a studio with rows of vertical racks for drying and storage of paintings.

She knocked at the door to the right of the original swinging doors that had been sealed and left as authentic-residual decoration. She heard nothing.

"Goddamn it," she yelled. "Answer the door." Her father was probably up. It was eleven o'clock, but his hours had been erratic since he had begun living alone in the barn.

"I'm busy," he called back from the silent interior.

She took out a letter-size fold-over brochure from her inside coat pocket.

"The promotion is in from New York."

"Leave it," he said. She heard the twang of a guitar string, the pitch mounting as a peg was screwed tighter. Then she heard the six disparate notes of an unharmonious chord. He had no ear for music. And he practiced often now, his foot tapping behind the beat of sixties rockers he played on a cassette recorder.

She opened the lid to a dark green painted tin mailbox, slipped the brochure in, and let the lid drop.

The Cottontail Inn conference room dining facility had only four windows on one side wall that gave little light, and the rheostats on the faux carriage lamps along the wall had to be cranked up to highest intensity. The room was set with white cloth-draped circular tables, and many of the seated women of the Rockton Garden Club had to turn their chairs to see Amanda on the small speaker's stage at the end of the room. A tubular reading light glowed on the podium next to the gooseneck mike. Amanda tilted up on her toes to see. She tapped the microphone with the middle finger of her right hand. The members had finished their chicken entrée, but still took a few seconds to direct their attention to Amanda.

"Welcome," Amanda said. She thanked Mertha Williams, the club President, for the success of the luncheon and the club. "The Ernest Goings Foundation has always been pleased to sponsor these quarterly meetings of the Garden Club," she continued, "and today's door prize is Ernest's new book of full color reproductions of his most popular paintings, 'Barn Doors in Lincoln County.' Mother, would you draw the winning slip?"

As her mother came forward, Amanda stood as tall as she could on her good leg to make a presence when she greeted her mother. This provincial crowd underappreciated Amanda, and some still thought her father really managed his art career. But it was Amanda's shrewd business skills that had anchored her father's success over the last ten years. She was not some nepotistic add on.

Amanda's mother, Margaret, selected one slip of paper from among many in a shoebox that was traditional for these drawings and brought forward by a volunteer. Margaret said nothing, and handed the winning slip to Amanda before returning to her seat.

And the winner? Tall and thin Fabia Worthington, who approached the podium without joy; she didn't like Ernest Goings' bucolic, hyper-realistic paintings, and adored Renoir. Amanda held the book-prize above her head for a few seconds for all to see before handing it to Fabia, who flipped through the pages. "No nudes?" she said. The audience laughed.

Amanda leaned closer to the microphone. "Fabia is kind to remind us that Ernest will show his new series of figure paintings next Thursday at the Slade Gallery in Boston on Newbury Street. Please join us." Then she walked back to her mother and her mother's friends, Julia and Sally, at a prominently placed table for four. Mertha gave the financial report and assigned committees for the spring garden show. Dessert was served.

"My goodness, Margaret," Sally whispered. "Thirteen nudes!"

"Ernest was always good at figure drawing," Margaret said. She had always been awed by his talent.

"Maine landscapes made him famous," Julia said smiling. "He should sow the seeds from plants that won last year's awards."

"It's his love of nature that makes his scenes come alive," Amanda said.

"Who knows what makes a painting good?" Sally said.

"He's always had a special gift," Margaret said.

"His art has touched millions," Amanda added.

"Not nudes," Sally said.

"They're portraits of a girl," Amanda said firmly.

"You can't judge the nudes," Julia said to Amanda. "You're all business."

"She is definitely a woman," Sally said. "You can see that." Sally picked up one of the brochures that had beenplaced at every table, showing a minute photo of one of the paintings; she waved it at Amanda. Julia nodded.

Amanda watched her mother closely. Margaret's eyes had lost focus, and she pushed her lower lip behind her upper teeth to control the trembling.

"I wouldn't trust my husband in the barn alone with a woman, clothed or unclothed," Julia said to Margaret. "How did you let him get away with it?"

"Her mother was with her," Margaret said emphatically.

"That's not what I heard," Julia said.

"Don't be catty," Amanda said. "She was only fifteen. Artists and models have strict professional standards."

Eunice, an indigent mother, had brought her daughter, Hester, for the early modeling sessions, until she found domestic work. After that, Hester went to the barn alone, disappearing over the ridge out of view.

"I'm sure it was her gift of holding still that attracted Ernest," Sally said sarcastically.

"That's not appropriate," said Amanda. These women were the foulest, most malevolent weeds of this community, and they made Amanda want to get out of rural Maine; she had an MBA – and national acclaim – and had job offers in D.C., Atlanta, and Oregon.

"You're too sensitive, Amanda," Julia said.

Amanda touched the arm of her mother for comfort. She had slumped in her chair, her eyes closed, no doubt hoping for a biting response to come to her to silence Sally and Julia.

"You're not still cooking for his sales, are you?" Julia asked Margaret.

Margaret leaned forward and clasped one hand in the other in her lap under the table to hide her tremor. "It wouldn't be a Goings' opening without our traditions," she said, bringing up her chin slightly. She baked sugar cookies shaped liked painters' palettes, with thumbholes and tan and brown chocolate chips along the edges that melted during cooking to suggest oil paints squeezed from a tube. She stacked the cookies on china platters on a linen-covered card table near the reception table at the door, far away from the catered opaque-eyed salmon, the bacon-wrapped warmed scallops, and the wedged sandwiches bulging with cold sprouts.

"It's a disgrace. After all you've done for him," Julia said.

Sally said. "He's treated you like dirt."

"Oh, Ernest loves it," Margaret said looking off into the distance. "And I do it for his fans. They expect it after all these years." Her voice was now shaky and her neck veins pulsing.

"Don't be a slave," Julia said. "It's embarrassing."

As Amanda stood, her chair scraped the bare wooden floors. She gripped her mother's arm. "We've got work to do," she said. She led her mother out of the inn.

⁂

When Amanda and Margaret reached home, Margaret refused Amanda's suggestion for coffee. She would not take her pills.

"They don't know art," Margaret said.

"They thrive on the salacious remark, Mother. No matter what the topic."

"He shouldn't have used the barn."

"It must have been innocent."

"No one believes that," Margaret said, and she lay face down on the sofa, weeping.

"They're not your friends, Mother," Amanda said. "Forget them."

Amanda ran the many branches of the Goings' business in her small, private, but well-appointed office at the family-owned gallery and art store in Rockton. She was reviewing the pricing for the show in Boston. Paintings sold at record prices in five or six figures, and Amanda turned enviable profits by negotiating the lowest commission for each painting.

It was Saturday, and Christina, who worked gallery sales on weekends, knocked on the office door.

"Eunice Cummings is here," she said. "She won't leave."

She was the model, Hester's, mother.

Amanda looked at an appointment book. "I could see her Tuesday afternoon at three."

But the door opened, and Eunice Cummings pushed Christina aside and walked in. "Got no time, Tuesday," she said.

"She wouldn't leave," Christina apologized.

Eunice stood in front of Amanda's desk, her hands in the pockets of her hand-knitted grey-green wool sweater, speechless. Her round face – spotted with facial hair on her chin and lip – had a grayish cast, her brown eyes looking down, her lips pursed.

"What can I do for you, Eunice?" Eunice was thin and her jeans hung loose. She wore a light green down jacket stitched in large squares, and a maroon woolen ski cap pulled down over her ears.

"Mrs. Pritchard said she'd get her son to take me and Hester to the opening in Boston," Eunice said.

The wealthy and stylish patrons on Newbury Street would probably hand Eunice a toilet brush and a mop when she walked into Slade Gallery. But the shows *were* open to the public. Amanda nodded. "You'll enjoy it," she said.

"I don't think so."

"Is there something specific you want, Eunice?"

"Hester wants her due," Eunice said.

Amanda leaned back in her swivel chair, her feet, in running shoes, dangling.

"He promised her ten percent of them paintings," Eunice said.

Amanda stared.

"He said he was going to treat her right."

Amanda breathed deeply. "Slow down, Eunice." Amanda swiveled a quarter turn in her chair, pushing with her leg. "Hester was paid the standard modeling fee. I've seen the cancelled checks."

"He showed her indecent, to my mind," Eunice said.

"You signed for the permission."

"Not for what is in that foldout."

"We don't pay a percentage of sales to a model," Amanda said. But previous models had always been clothed, old, sturdy people who wore hats to block the sun or catch the rain, and always at a distance, on the porch of a farmhouse or on the dock with commercial fishing boats in the background.

"I got a lawyer. An esquire. He's going to write you a letter. I just come to see if you'd do right without us paying him all that money."

Ten percent was at least three hundred thousand dollars. Eunice remained standing, waiting for an answer.

"He told her lies," Eunice continued.

Amanda's father was capable of avoiding truth, usually by prolonged, miserable silences.

"He said he loved her."

"You heard him?"

"Hester don't lie."

Eunice stared at her unblinking, and a tear trickled down her face to the left of her nose.

Amanda had to be practical. "I'd be careful about spreading rumors, Eunice."

Eunice didn't hesitate. "Ain't never been one to talk bad about folks. Never."

"Well, don't get your hopes up. We are not paying a percentage of sales." Eunice's gaze went distant, somewhere behind Amanda. She was trembling with frustration. When words failed, she left the office breathing hard and fast.

Amanda dismissed Christina. Her heart was still pounding, and she sat with her head back, her eyes closed. After a few minutes, she called artists she knew well and confirmed their hourly rates for models, never with residual compensations. Then she itemized every check and cash withdrawal marked for modeling fees. Hester had definitely been paid more than required by common practice. For the last sessions, it seemed sometimes she was given, by Ernest, excessive compensation for time spent, and without a reason noted in the "for" column.

Amanda knocked on the front door of the barn-studio, and when there was no answer, she tried the knob. It was unlocked. Her father rarely answered the studio door, and never when he was painting. A thirty-six by fifty-two inch canvas primed with a burnt umber/ raw sienna wash was mounted, and totally dry, on his prime easel. He was at his workbench stretching canvas over handmade stretchers. Two canvasses freshly gessoed were propped against the wall. He prepared daily, but he hadn't finished a painting since he stopped painting Hester. Amanda closed the door.

"We need to talk," Amanda said.

"Well, hello to you," he said.

"Cut that off," Amanda said, nodding at the boom box on the workbench.

He looked briefly to Amanda then back to his work, irritated, as if Amanda were an inferior model begging for work.

Amanda pushed the off toggle-switch on the player.

"Eunice Cummings came to me today. She expects ten percent of sales of the Hester portraits."

"She's deranged," he said, looking away from her and picking up ridged canvas-pliers from a workbench. He gripped the edge of the linen canvas.

"You never promised?"

"I never talked to her after the first few sessions. She stopped coming." He fastened the canvas, seven sharp hits from a pneumatic staple-gun.

"She says you told Hester."

He looked sharply at her. "Don't bring Hester into it." He leaned the canvas on edge against the leg under the table.

"You painted her!"

He walked to a large picture window to look out, his hands clasped behind his head. "Hester is off limits, Amanda. None of your business."

She moved to where he could not ignore her.

"Eunice has a lawyer. Hester *is* my business."

"Eunice is lying." His breathing was shallow. "She took the modeling fees."

"Everyone in town thinks something happened in the barn."

He walked two steps away from Amanda. She could see only his backside.

"Don't accuse me."

"I'm asking for the truth."

"You're prying."

Amanda grabbed his arm but he refused to turn. "What did you do?"

"Don't be a bitch. I painted a girl. And I did it well."

She let go and moved back, still facing him.

"We've handed out the brochure. Nudes, they said. Not child figure studies."

"Those sessions were hard work, Amanda. I spent more than a year finally doing something more than rocks and curtains blowing through an open window."

"You painted a fifteen year-old girl alone with you in a barn. We all wonder about that."

"I captured that beautiful balance between innocence and sexuality. Nobody alive has done what I've done."

Paintings were a product to Amanda. She never studied her father's paintings. She had no idea what an artist or an art critic would think.

He walked to the small refrigerator near a sink set in a small counter top. He bent over and took a soda. He turned to Amanda, sweeping with his free hand long, uneven strands of gray hair with dark streaks from his face. His blues eyes, now more faded watercolor than the rich cobalt oil-paint blue of his youth, fixed on the wall above and behind Amanda. He drank from the can.

"A scandal could end your career," she said.

"Hester will never accuse. Trust me. She's not the type." He smiled.

"Our fame and fortune are at stake here."

He grimaced, shaking his head. "Manage the business, Amanda. That's what you're good at." Then he stepped on the trashcan foot-pedal; the lid raised, and he tossed the can, which disappeared. "I'm an artist. Hester was a model. No one needs to know more."

"I'm not sure I can bury this."

"We're already in the money. Marty's presold four of the nudes. They're exceptional."

"Not if the circumstances are clouded by suspicion."

"Great art is great art. It moves people in different ways."

He looked at her as if she were a gnarled downed tree limb that needed to be removed from the yard. What did he want in a daughter?

"Well. Don't ignore Mother at the reception," Amanda said, buttoning her coat. "You at least owe her that."

She let herself out the door.

⁂

Hester Cummings did seasonal counterwork at the cold-serve lobster-roll shack in Wiscasset. She left work and met Amanda outside on a path a few feet from the low highway bridge spanning the Sheepscot River. She had kept Amanda waiting for half an hour.

"Are you still modeling?" Amanda asked when they stood together. Hester was close to five-feet five, and Amanda tilted her head back slightly to see Hester's vacant face with uneasy eyes.

"The lawyer said I shouldn't talk to you," Hester said.

"To me? Or anyone?"

"He said you'd be the one asking me questions." Hester stared at Amanda, her hands, palm in, tucked in the back pockets of her tight jeans skirt. She had put on weight.

"But you're talking to me."

"I didn't like him too good."

When Hester smiled a little, Amanda smiled too. Amanda's smile was her best feature. She felt cheated on good features. Her hair was scraggly and a dull brown, and a childhood pox had pitted her skin with scars. But her smile made people relax, and speak more freely.

"Did my father promise more than a modeling fee, Hester?"

"He said I meant a lot to him."

"Did he say he loved you?"

Hester hesitated. "Yes, ma'am."

"He doesn't paint you anymore. You okay with that?"

"He got done with his series."

"You still see him?"

Hester looked away.

"And you think he'll do you right?"

"Course he will. When he can." She straightened and her head went back defiantly. She glared down at Amanda.

For a while, Amanda looked at a lobster boat coming to dock. Then she looked back at Hester. "Do you love him?"

Hester squeezed her eyes shut for a few seconds, but didn't answer.

"Did he say he'd pay you ten percent?"

"That's what he said I was worth."

Amanda leaned a few inches closer. "It's hard to believe, Hester. We've never promised that to a model."

Hester looked away again. "You wouldn't know about modeling. You ain't that pretty."

They stood in silence. Although Hester had matured early to a soft, almost plump fertility, she stood with her head slightly down, her toes turned in, her arms hanging awkwardly like a child. And, despite what she thought, being young was her only asset. She must have thrived on the attention from posing. How real posing must have made her feel; Ernest's constant stares for discovery made her needy and wondrous, submissive and hungry. Was Hester in love with her father? Or was she just curious about men?

"I loved a man," Amanda said. "I couldn't be without him."

"I heard about him. He left you."

"In a way. He killed himself," Amanda said. When Amanda was in the MBA program in Boston, she had loved the brilliant but sullen Jimmy Headman. His lovemaking still haunted her. She had not found anyone like him.

"Loving hurts a lot, don't it? I mean, like it isn't all feeling good."

"He went to take care of his demented mother in Canada."

"Look. I ain't saying no more," Hester said. "Lawyer said you'd try to trick me."

She turned toward the shack.

"I won't trick you," Amanda said wearily.

"You're tough as nails, Miss Amanda. I can't trust you."

Amanda shook her head as Hester turned and walked away. "Most people don't feel that way," she said when Hester couldn't hear.

Amanda waited until Hester disappeared back into the shack, then she turned to gaze at the water. Colorful buoys marking submerged lobster traps bobbed on the wind-whipped surface. The water was dark grey.

Early on the day of the opening, Amanda parked in the drive of her mother's house. It was biting cold in the mornings now, and the two oaks on each side of her parents' house had dropped the last of their brown shriveled leaves. Amanda helped her mother load groceries, linens and the folding card table into the car. Her mother shivered in a light green dress and a skimpy raincoat that she thought was her most attractive outfit since she'd lost thirteen pounds.

Amanda drove. They traveled in silence through small towns until they got to Brunswick. They stopped at a Dunkin' Donuts for coffee and doughnuts that they ate in the car.

"Did you talk to him?" Margaret picked small bits of a plain cake-donut with her thumb and forefinger. She would eat less than a third – throw the rest away.

Amanda did not answer. Her father took up too much precious space in their lives that he didn't deserve.

"He was improper?" Margaret persisted.

"He's such an asshole. He's never been open about anything."

Margaret put her doughnut and half-filled small coffee cup into a bag.

"You talked to the girl," Margaret said.

"She loves him," Amanda replied. "But I can't prove she screwed him."

"I'm in the way of their happy life together?"

"She's filled with need and wonder, Mother. I doubt she thinks about you."

Amanda placed her trash in the bag and climbed out of the car to deposit it in a barrel. She got back in and started the car without replying.

"Don't you think she's retarded?" Margaret said.

"She's shy, mother. And afraid. But she's not evil. I feel sorry for her."

They were soon on the I-95 south for Boston. Margaret sat with her hands flat on her thighs staring ahead at the traffic.

"He should never have painted her," Margaret said after they passed the tollbooth.

"He gave her a sense of self she'd never known," Amanda said. "And probably will never know again."

"I called Angus Partridge. Sex with a minor is illegal whether it gave her a sense of self or not."

Amanda passed an eighteen-wheeler. She liked to keep exactly five miles an hour above the speed limit. Amanda didn't care if her mother was talking to Angus about divorce proceedings, but she dreaded the battle. Margaret stared ahead as if some rock wall would emerge on the highway and end their lives.

"I don't think he's finished one canvas since he stopped painting that girl," Margaret said softly.

"He thinks the success of the show will override the suspicions," Amanda said. "And if he did have sex with her, I doubt Hester would ever testify, or that he'd ever be successfully prosecuted even if charged." But even if the show were a success and Ernest went on unscathed by opinions, the marriage was over. Amanda felt a new resolve to never marry.

Amanda steered the car into the fast lane. Maybe a quick settlement with Eunice would be necessary to cut off the publicity as soon as possible.

"He's only good at barn doors," Margaret said.

Amanda meter-parked on the street in Boston and helped her mother carry ingredients and utensils to the gallery. The front door to the showroom was locked – the gallery was closed two days for instillation of the new show – and Amanda used her key to enter the side door. In the kitchen, Margaret stored cookie dough in the refrigerator, turned on one of three baking ovens to preheat, and washed two bowls for cheese straws. They had a few hours before the caterers arrived at five-thirty.

"I want to see the show before I bake," Margaret said.

"I'll meet you in the gallery," Amanda said, and she walked to the small room she used as an office during shows. She took a manila folder out of her briefcase and carried it to the showroom to confirm inventory.

Her mother had turned on the lights. Amanda had seen only a few of the paintings; her visits to the barn were for business, and the few canvasses she had seen were partially finished. Now the nudes were prominently mounted in gold leaf frames with traditional Goings' landscapes in between.

"Mama?" Amanda said.

Her mother slumped on a side chair, staring. She pointed to a life-sized frontal view of Hester gazing wide-eyed from the canvas. Hester's buttocks splayed over the edge a porcelain sink, her hands on the edge for support. Both feet were spread apart and flat on the floor. She dominated the space with detail – every hair seemed recreated, flecks on her blue irises were plain and disturbing, the healed acne scars of her facial skin, uncompromised. Her nudity exposed a strange asymmetry of the nipples on her large breasts. Her pelvis was too wide for beauty, and her sturdy legs ended in thick ankles. Her facial expression seemed unaware that anyone would look at her. He had captured the childishness of her figure, and an almost prepubescent softness of her face, but the overall impression was not that she was child – or nude. Rather, it showed the excessive time and passion of the artist to create such minutia.

"It's lewd," her mother said. "It's like he licked every inch of that girl's skin."

Amanda agreed, but said nothing. The adjacent paintings were half and three quarter studio figures, smaller and less offensive. Then there were two outdoor poses in spring settings, one where Hester lay face up in grass with her hands behind her head; in the other, she squatted to pick up a flower.

Amanda moved and stopped in front of a life-size portrait of Hester sitting on a wooden bench in front of a piano – a quarter-turn view – her arms back, her left leg extended to the floor. Her right leg was bent at the knee with her foot on the bench, a suggestive glimpse of her privates nestled between pink thigh-flesh. Amanda moaned; such detail seemed so unnecessary.

"I hate him," her mother said. "He wanted her."

Amanda gripped her mother's shoulders from the back and pushed her to standing.

"Forget him. Finish the baking," Amanda said. She still hoped the meticulous images would awe the patrons enough to ignore her father's obsession, which, Amanda was now convinced, was more lust than love.

"He's making a fool of himself. And he's your father," her mother said.

"They might be art, Mother."

"They're filthy," her mother said.

Amanda followed her mother into the kitchen, opened the refrigerator, took a bowl and placed it in her mother's hands. "I've got work with Marty."

Amanda walked down the short hall to one of three office doors. She knocked.

Marty, the gallery owner, greeted her from behind his desk, but did not smile. "Ready?" he asked.

Amanda took a folder for documents from a leather briefcase and placed it on the desk. Marty glanced at each paper.

"Will this ruin his career?" Amanda asked as he read. "My mother thinks it's artistic suicide."

"I tried. I joked with him, said they looked like Mexican porn on velvet. He said I was a shitty agent."

"It's all profit for you, Marty."

"Who cares if they're immoral? They'll sell, Amanda. Go into private collections. Look at Balthus."

Marty moved out from behind his desk. He was bald and wore a pinstriped business suit and a white shirt open at the neck.

Together they went out the gallery side door and walked two blocks to a lawyer's office that was up a flight of stairs above a woman's clothing store, and notarized the sales agreements.

"I'm going home," said Marty when they were back at the door. "Pick you up at the motel?"

"We'll dress here." They had two hours before the caterers and personnel arrived. More than three hours before the opening.

Amanda let herself into the gallery and went into the kitchen. She placed her briefcase on the floor. She called out to her mother, who did not answer. The smell of baking cookies forced memories of summer vacation days home from boarding school, her mother hosting her father's openings, and a joyful celebration in an outrageously expensive restaurant to celebrate her father's growing success.

She walked out, the door closing behind her.

"Mother!" she called.

Silence.

She walked to the gallery. Her mother sat in a wooden arm chair in the empty expanse of the show space, her feet splayed before her, her arms draped over the sides, her head back with her eyes closed.

Amanda felt her mother's pulse.

"Go away," her mother moaned. Amanda turned on the lights. She gasped.

An open plastic bottle of Liquid-Plumer lay on its side in an opaque pool that corroded the varnish on the oak floors. Two brushes and a kitchen fork on a kitchen towel were nearby.

"My God, Mother."

"It's the stuff to unclog drains," she said, her eyes still closed. "I got tired."

Every Hester detail was scraped clean from the sink portrait.

"He's beyond saving himself," her mother said.

Amanda paused. Margaret had left the background of the painting meticulously preserved, accenting Ernest Goings' talent for settings. The remaining nudes seemed even more out of place now. For minutes, Amanda did not move.

"That poor child."

"We can't judge," Amanda said.

"We might keep him out of jail."

Amanda scanned the remaining nudes. She had never felt about paintings. Feelings corroded a manager's business acumen in the art world. But she knew what her mother felt. There was more than bad judgment on these canvasses. There was revelation.

Amanda bent over and handed a brush to her mother. "Start on the last three over there," she said. "We'll meet in the middle."

Amanda found another paintbrush and a spatula in the kitchen, and two bottles of caustic under the sink. Back in the gallery, her broad brushstrokes dissolved paint on contact. She did not preserve settings.

They worked in silence for almost an hour, scraping off what remained of Hester until she was gone from every portrait. Margaret gasped when Marty came into the gallery. Amanda collected her tools and set them on a chair.

"Goddamn it," Marty said, his face creased with lines, his eyes dark and threatening. "You've really fucked up."

The odor of burnt cookies seeped into the gallery from the kitchen. Amanda suppressed a smile.

"Oh dear . . ." Margaret sighed sarcastically. "The cookies."

"Burnt to an inedible crisp . . ." Amanda said.

"What will the guest have to enjoy?" Margaret said, with uncharacteristic sarcasm.

"It's a crime," Marty said. He stood with his feet planted, the fingers in his clenched fists turning white.

"It's a family matter," Amanda said. "Back off."

Technically, the paintings were Marty's property during the sale.

"You're going to put me in jail? Put Mother on the chain gang?"

"Insurance will be tricky, Amanda."

"It's an act of God." Amanda laughed. True, Marty was not a pleasant man, overweight with his handsome features sliding away, but he worked hard with dependable honesty. She looked at him. He was frowning.

"I have expenses," Marty said.

"You've made more than two million off Ernest Goings," Amanda said.

"I've got my girls to educate."

"Hang loose, Marty. I'll cover your losses."

Marty sighed and stared at the two women streaked with dissolving paint: one with a skinny but muscular body with a deformed leg and the hard face of a woman who knows pain, her brown eyes glinting with excitement; the other teetering on old age, but breathing fast and grinning with the broad innocence of a child. For years, he had disliked

Ernest Goings and ignored the family whenever he could, but now his face held no anger.

Amanda took her mother's hand to leave.

"The pans. My purse," her mother said.

"Get out of Boston," Marty said. "This has to be reported."

Amanda and Margaret went to the kitchen to collect their things, the double-hinged door closing behind them.

The doorbell rang persistently. Marty unlocked the gallery front door. Eunice stood in a green cotton dress, printed with white and yellow daisies, that buttoned down the front. One brown lace in her white running shoes had come untied. Next to her, Hester wore black jeans tight enough to stretch the buttonhole at the waist, and a too big, thrift-store white blouse with an Alice-in-Wonderland frilly trim. She teetered in silver stiletto-heeled pumps. Her ankles were swollen.

"We're closed," Marty said.

"This here is the model," Eunice said. "We can't do the regular time . . ."

"I'm sorry," Marty interjected.

". . . our ride got to leave early."

Eunice wedged her way in through the door opening and dragged Hester behind her.

"We got our rights," Eunice said.

Marty held out his arm to block them. Eunice pushed his arm away and he didn't resist.

Eunice strode by and Hester wobbled, hurrying to keep up. They stopped in mid gallery.

Amanda came alone from the kitchen and Marty pointed to Eunice and Hester. Hester took small steps to stand alone in front of the portrait Margaret had mutilated first. She whimpered.

After more than a minute, Hester touched her forefinger to the edge of the hole in the canvas. Then, with a flat palm, she intently stroked the air where her image had been, as if she could wipe off the reality of the hole and restore the illusion. She choked and let her hand fall to her side.

"I was important to him," Hester said.

Amanda cringed.

"I wasn't just a picture," Hester said. She sat on the floor, cross-legged. The waist-button on her jeans had popped open. One shoe fell off and lay on its side, the heel angled up. Hester stared at the hole where she had once been so meticulously rendered.

Amanda walked back to the kitchen. Margaret held her purse and her utensils.

"It was the child, wasn't it?" Margaret said. "Was her mother with her?"

"She's destroyed."

Amanda led her out the side door to the car, and in half an hour they were driving directly to Margaret's sister's house in New Hampshire, arriving well after midnight to stay the night.

"I'll send your things," Amanda said to her mother the next morning.

"What about the house?"

"Don't go back. I'll come for you in a few weeks."

"And Ernest?"

"He'll probably press charges, Mother."

Amanda drove straight to the Rockton office. She taped an "Out of Business" sign to the window. She secured valuables, mailed deposits, disconnected phones, paid bills. She went to the bank to certify a check for Marty's commission. She closed business accounts, took her due, and transferred money for her mother's private accounts. She had accepted a position as CFO of a commercial gallery in Oregon.

In her final hour in Rockton, Amanda placed all the documentation of Hester's modeling and payments with promotional photos of the destroyed portraits, in protective sleeves, in a business envelope for mailing. She dialed Portland police.

"I'm reporting abuse of a minor."

"You the victim?"

She faltered. "No," she said. She took a deep breath. "I'm the daughter."

"You got evidence?"

"Talk to the victim. I think she's pregnant."

CROSSING OVER

My name is Agnes Swaggert and I work in this nursing home for next to nothing. I do good things for old folks like Mr. Wiggins who has been with us for two months. He lost his hair to radiation, his eyesight to Cadillacs, and his voice to a trach. He moans non-stop, drools and spits, shits five times a day so the sheets got to be changed. I don't think he ever sleeps.

I go to sit for a moment at the nurses' station, put my arms on the counter. I got scars on my right arm, and I set to thinking, as I often do when I feel like this. Them scars make me think about my kin – grandma mostly. Mr. Wiggins moans but I pay him no mind. Mr. Wiggins will be number fifty-nine.

Funny how I can see every one of them. I think goodly about each one, being as I knew them so well. Like being down front in the movie theater and the lights go on and you turn around and there they are lined up row after row. Sometimes I think I'm a mother duck, all of them waddling behind me, crossing over the road to the other side. Mr. Wiggins is whining real good now, so I think about Grandma. What the woman she was. I'd be guessing I liked her more than momma or daddy.

It was my granny who taught me, after momma had left for work and it was bed time.

"What is that grandma?" I said to her one night.

"You're mother will never teach you."

"No. No. What's in your hand?" I had expected she had a peppermint stick hidden for me. But it was only a cigarette. She lit up, took out the cigarette from her lips, and picked a piece of tobacco from her tongue.

"When can I smoke?" I asked.

"When you're old enough to know what's right and wrong."

"I know what's right and wrong," I said.

"You don't no-how. Your Momma ain't teaching you the ways of Lord."

"She told me, Grandma! She told me how Jesus had this fish and when lots of people come, he kept cutting up the fish and he fed a whole crowd. And then they wanted bread, and Jesus had this loaf that when you sliced it just kept coming until everyone weren't hungry no more."

"It's the suffering, precious," she said. "That's where the real learning is. Jesus taught us to suffer unto me. It's the suffer part you're mamma don't know nothing about. She's Godless and I ain't going to tell you about it so don't ask."

"You mean 'cause Daddy left?"

"I don't know's I blame your mother, what with her troubles and all. You too young to understand."

"She taught me, grandma. She did!"

"We must know ourselves," grandma said. "Jesus went into the dark and it was hot and dry and he stayed there for a long time like none of us could. And when they put them spikes through his hands and feet. He never cried out once. Never!"

"I know," I said, but I really wasn't sure.

"You don't know nothing," she said. "I can make you into a real woman."

"I'd like that," I said.

"Hold out your arm," Grandma said.

I did as she commanded, putting out my arm, pulling back my nighty sleeve.

"Sit up on the edge of the bed," she said.

I shifted my legs so they hung over the side.

"Don't you flinch," she said. She took two strong draws on a cigarette till it was glowing and she put the tip on the white part of my arm and pressed down. The pain went shooting up, not like lightning, but like when you get a finger shut in the door. I sat there looking at grandma and never flinched, never cried. Grandma counted.

"One. Two. Three. Four. Five." Then she pulled the cigarette away. "That was real good," she said. "Real good. Now we do one more time tonight."

And over the next month I got to know how Jesus, our Savior, handled the pain, 'cause he was like God's son and it made him special. I got to where Grandma could count five or six times. "Real good," she said, "I's proud of you. You is a good learner."

Well, old Mr. Wiggins is alone again now. I wait till after the night shift comes on. The only nurse is on the second floor. I can hear when she moves; it's so quiet at night except for Mr. Wiggins whiney moan. Loud, he is tonight, bless his soul. Past being able to suffer like a real Christian. He moaning like a heathen now.

I don't need my medicine syringe for this. I just take away the breathing machine, hold my hand over his mouth, and pinch his nose. I got sterile gloves on, of course. He's in restraints and at first he wiggles like a fish out of water on a dry dock. Then, in three minutes it's over. I put the breathing machine back on.

"God bless you," I say to Mr. Wiggins as he is crossing over. "God bless you."

I go out and clean up Mrs. Sampson. She's got bladder problems.

"How you making it?" I say to her.

She tries to smile. I like that. Even though she's suffering, it's like she ain't giving in.

"Could you get me some water, Agnes?" she says.

I look at her. "Don't you fret, dear. I bring the water soon as I drop Mr. Wiggins dirty sheets by the laundry."

"Hurry," she said.

I can tell you this, I heard the first sound of whine in her voice, the first sign of her not taking her suffering like the good Christian woman she used to be.

THE ACTIVIST

"I ain't going to stand for it," Mama said. She said this often.

She held a small dead human about as long as an ear of corn. Even though the head was too big, the hands too small, you could tell it might have been somebody.

"Push down," Mama said.

My sister moaned. With a gush of blood the afterbirth slid onto the bed. Her skin was white as wood ash.

"I don't feel good," she said.

"Shut up, Pearl Anne," Mama said. "Shut up and grow up."

"I'm seventeen."

"You're acting like a two-year-old."

"I'm going to throw up," Pearl Anne said.

I wasn't feeling so hot either.

"Go get some towels, Ether Mae. Help get Pearl Anne cleaned up."

I didn't move. Pearl Anne got herself into this fix, not me. I'd never had a boy put his thing into me. Pearl Anne said it felt funny but not so good that she couldn't do without it. So she'd decided to quit. She wanted more respect. She quit too late.

Now Mama moaned and held this dead thing. "My grandchild," she said. "Didn't I tell you get some towels?"

"Don't want to." I backed away a little.

"You'll get the stick. You're too old to have me telling you what to do." I was eleven.

I found some rags and two towels and got them wet under the faucet in the sink, then squeezed the water out.

"Goddamn it. Wring them out. You're dripping all over the floor," Mama screamed.

"What's that doctor's name wouldn't treat you, Pearl Anne?"

Pearl Anne put her hand to her mouth and wiped away some vomit chunks. "Lady doctor."

I started wiping up blood on the bed. I picked up the afterbirth, holding it between two towels so I wouldn't have to touch it, but I could still feel the warmth. I dropped it in the toilet and flushed it down. I got Pearl Anne on the potty. She still had lots of blood that came out in chunks like sliced cow's liver. Her belly skin was pale with blue veins snaking around.

While I worked to get the blood off Pearl Anne, Mama sat at the kitchen table. She had a shoebox. She took a face cloth, pink with a white border, and laid it in the bottom. Then she put Pearl Anne's dead thing inside. She took a piece of Saran wrap and covered the top so you could still see Pearl Anne's dead thing's little face and hands and its legs all drawn up. Mama put the top on the box and took a black felt-tip Magic Marker and smeared in tight strokes with lines next to each other so the entire box top was black.

"What's that, Mama?"

"A coffin."

I thought she was a little crazy from losing her only grandchild. "It's a shoebox," I mumbled.

She whacked me across the side of my head half-hard, but still serious.

"Don't want no disrespect for the dead. This is kin."

"What kin?"

"Your nephew."

I stared hard but didn't feel any kinship.

Mama pushed me ahead of her into the bedroom. Pearl Anne's bed was wet and still stained with blood.

"She's got blood in her crotch," Mama yelled.

"I ain't doing that," I said. So we decided to put Pearl Anne in the bathtub. The water heater wasn't working right and I had to heat water on the stove. Mama and I got Pearl Anne in the tub.

"I'm going to faint. I'm going to faint," Pearl Anne whined loud and ornery.

After we washed her, I helped her out of the tub and Mama led her to my bed. She fell asleep. Snoring.

"Come with me," Mama said.

"What about Pearl Anne?"

"Only one thing wrong with her; she can't say no."

Mama climbed into the pickup on the driver's side, setting the little shoebox on the seat. After I got in she said, "Don't let it slide onto the floor."

I put my hand on the box and turned it so it was long against the back of the seat. I imagined the ink stain on my fingers.

Mama drove dead stop to forty-five to dead stop. She blasted the horn at people walking in the road, at old people driving too slow. She breathed scratchy and deep. Her blazing eyes reflected light from the windshield as if her eye globes were marbles, and her hands gripped the wheel so hard her scruffy red fingers were white at the joints.

"Where we going?" I asked.

"Watch the coffin. You'll see soon enough."

We drove over the Chattahoochee River Bridge, past the old mill with the missing roof and broken windows, then the abandoned railway station. The *We Care* health clinic was at the mini mall just ahead.

Mama stopped a block away where a pay telephone was tacked to the wall of the 7-Eleven store. She dialed 911 and the local TV station. Mama got back in the truck and sighed. "I bet they won't come."

"Why you do that, Mama?"

"Shut your mouth. We doing what's right for our family." She grabbed my hair and yanked my head so my face was looking right at her. "You got to fight for every bit of justice in this world. Don't ever make me say that to you again."

"Let go."

"You don't deserve to be a Crawford."

I wished I wasn't a Crawford. Or a kid. Or living in that doublewide trailer with Pearl Anne and Mama. But I kept my mouth zipped tight.

Mama got the truck started, and in thirty seconds she double-parked in front of the clinic even though there were other spots open. "You grab the coffin," she said.

We got out of the truck and marched into the clinic. Doctor's names were spelled out in white plastic letters on a black felt board. A star marked the "physician of the day,"—a woman doctor.

"Follow me." Mama yanked my arm so hard I almost dropped the box.

We marched right by the receptionist into the back.

The woman doctor stood writing at a chest-high counter. Both the doctor and the nurse looked at us.

"You the doctor?" Mama said to the woman. She said "dock-tooor." Mean-like.

"Doctor Paterson."

"A real doctor?"

Mama pushed me forward.

"Yes."

"You got ALL the training or are you IN training."

"I'm a special fellow..."

"Ah! If you was ALL trained my grandchild would be with us today."

"You've got your facts..."

"Give me that box," Mama screamed at me.

I shoved the box forward thinking Mama would take it.

"Take off the lid" she said instead.

I could see magic marker all over my fingers and I had a sinking feeling it would never come off.

"Turn that lid upside down." Mama grabbed the box so the doctor could see through the Saran wrap. "This child is dead because of you."

The doctor stared like the grandchild might breathe fire or rise from the dead. I could see her hands tremble.

"My daughter, Ms. Pearl Anne Crawford, seen you day before yesterday. You told her go to the welfare hospital."

The nurse sitting behind a desk tried to speak up but her mouth was working like a dying fish on a dry dock in the hot sun. "We can't take Medicaid," the doctor said. "I checked her. She was all right."

"She weren't all right. Her baby died."

"She was fine. This girl was with her." The doctor pointed down at me scary, like God from the stained glass window in my Mama's Church of the Apocalypse.

I started to say Pearl Anne was fine when the doctor saw her but Mama bumped me with an elbow before I could finish.

"I referred her to the County Hospital," the doctor said.

Mama hated the County Hospital worse than she hated sinners. "We ain't never going to that hell hole," Mama went on. "You made my daughter grieve."

I thought of Pearl Anne snoring on my bed.

The nurse whispered to the doctor. "I'm calling the cops."

"That's good. We need some arrests here," Mama said.

A man and woman from 911 rushed from the lobby through the inner door carrying bags and metal tubes and a little tank. "Emergency?"

"Goddamn right there's an emergency." Mama peeked out the open door looking for the TV crew.

"Where?"

"Give me that coffin, Ether Mae." I handed over the coffin. My nephew now was on his side, his arms still out and touching the cardboard like he might be trying to get out. Mama twisted the coffin so the 911 people could see.

"Dead."

"It's a fetus," the 911 woman said.

"Kilt. Refused treatment. Put that in your report. By her." Mama pointed an accusing finger at the doctor, who was shaking all over now and looking angry with Mama.

"Weren't her fault, Mama." The doctor had treated Pearl Anne really kind.

Mama hit me so hard I dropped the coffin. The Saran wrap came off one side and my nephew rolled out on the floor, ashamed, I thought, of being naked and paraded around by Mama.

"You dropped our kin." She hit me again. Softer, but it still hurt.

Mama peered out to see about the TV people. But cops with black uniforms and caps with shiny plastic bills came in, a white guy tall as an apple tree and a skinny little Black lady.

"What's the matter?" the big cop said.

The nurse spoke up quick. "It's her." She pointed to Mama. "Brought a dead fetus and says we're responsible. Threatening us."

"I didn't threaten no one. I want them arrested."

"For what?" the woman cop asked.

"Killing my grandchild. Making my daughter grieve. Going against the will of God!"

I could tell there were a lot of feelings whizzing around that room, but no sympathy, not for Mama. The 911 people looked at Mama as if she were a lunatic. The nurse and receptionist thought, "white trash." The doctor still shook with anger. Both cops stared at Mama, wondering why they ever went to cop school and planning what to do next.

"Can you take that baby?" the big cop asked the 911 guys.

"I can't take a dead fetus we ain't treated."

"Against regulations to keep it here," the nurse said.

"You ain't doing nothing with my grandchild."

"Did you treat this woman's daughter, Doctor?" the lady cop asked.

The doctor gripped the edge of the counter with both hands. "I checked her but didn't charge her."

"No-pays!" the receptionist said. I scooped up my nephew with the side of the coffin box and settled him inside. His head was twisted on his neck a little like he might have been hurt.

"The baby was alive," continued the doctor. "It moved."

"Nothing wrong?" the cop asked.

"Blood pressure up a little. I suggested the County Hospital."

"We can't accept Medicaid," the receptionist said.

"Look here, Dr. Smart Girl," Mama spat, "we ain't never going to the County."

"That's where we work," said the 911 woman.

"Well, let me tell you. The devil's got you. My husband, Horace Crawford, God rest his soul, sat with blood pressure and diabetes and his heart failed so bad you could see it thumping in his chest. He went to your County Hospital; I was sitting beside him, waiting for nine hours. Every time I walked up to the counter they told me they'd get to him as soon as they could. Well, they got to him. But by then he was as a cold as a slab of hog hanging in a chill room."

"That's too bad," said the 911 woman.

"Criminal," said Mama. And she was crying tears. Pearl Anne said crying was when Mama was at her best. The people here didn't know what to think. The 911 guys looked like they'd just seen the ghost of my papa.

"He wouldn't have been cold. Takes a long time to get cold," the 911 man said.

"He was dead. Dead cold," Mama said in a voice so controlled and angry the 911 man looked out the door to avoid the hatred in her stare.

The police told 911 to get on, and they sat Mama down in a chair in the waiting room. "I know you're distressed," said the woman cop, "but you're out of line here. My partner wants to book you."

"I ain't done nothing."

"Disturbing the peace. But I told him to let you go."

"They kilt my grandchild."

"They did what was right. Now you get on."

I sat in a waiting room chair holding the coffin on my lap. Mama was thinking about what she could do.

"I ain't moving until you arrest them."

"I mean it. Move along or you go to jail."

"Go to the truck, Ether Mae."

"And take that dead thing with you," spat the nurse.

"Watch your words," the woman cop warned the nurse as I started out.

A few minutes later, the cops shoved Mama out the door.

As soon as we got home, Mama went to pray at the Church of the Apocalypse and talk to her friends about a demonstration at the clinic, probably burning candles and a protest fire. "You keep your nephew safe," she said as she left, and I sat at the kitchen table looking through the Saran wrap at my kin. He seemed like he was trying to catch his breath so I took off the Saran wrap. He liked that, I thought. I smiled at him, 'cause he was so small and helpless. "You came at the wrong time," I said. "For you," I added. I thought for a moment. "But sure was the right time for Mama." I thought he might have smiled a little.

Pearl Anne was still asleep in my room. I just sat with my nephew for a while. He seemed so nice all balled up and laying on his back on the pink-and-white facecloth little blanket. I got thinking about respect . . . him being dropped in the clinic and falling out of his coffin and all. About being gawked at naked under his Saran wrap. And I thought, it ain't right. "You only got me," I said to him. I knew he was dead, but he heard. I was sure of it. "You need help."

I turned my little nephew in his coffin so he was comfortable on his side. I got four stones the size of chicken eggs from the garden and put one in each corner. Then I put the Saran wrap back on top. The lid was torn, but I made it whole with Scotch tape. With the same roll of tape, I sealed the coffin lid on tight and put it in a plastic grocery sack.

I walked, holding the coffin flat so the rocks wouldn't move, to the Chattahoochee River. I'd heard Chattahoochee was some Indian god. Probably had long pigtails and feathers stuck in his hair. Even though the Indians I'd seen never smiled much, I thought Little Nephew would be happier with them than he would with us. I walked to where the highway crossed over, along the guardrail to the center of the flat bridge, and let the bag with my nephew in his coffin fall into the water.

Plop. The coffin floated away from the bridge and disappeared where the river and the sky were the same shade of dark.

I closed my eyes. I could see my little smiling nephew sitting in my papa's lap at the right hand of God. Those Chattahoochee Indians had taken him home.

THE PERENNIAL STUDENT

Associate Professor William Possum was looking for student Denise Witherspoon, this attractive, slightly overweight, moderately intelligent woman who was destroying his class. Denise had caused five angry letters, two dropouts, and a formal complaint that said she "made an evening of anticipated learning a dreadful experience."

And it had gone farther than the classroom. Possum's mentor and department chair, Alice Cherry, had made it clear she was "damn tired" of the "deteriorating" situation.

"She's impossible," Possum had countered, and he described Denise's undeserved pride and unjust criticism of her fellow students.

Finally, in frustration, Possum had argued Denise should be dismissed. "Give her her money back," he said. He was shocked at Cherry's lack of understanding. Students paid good money and were entitled to their education, Cherry said. "This is an administrative problem. Talk to her!" Possum had to talk to Denise alone before she got to the classroom.

Possum waited inside the entrance hall of the ivy-coated building that housed the Departments of English and Computer Science. He had a direct view of the front, although he made sure those coming in could not make out his features in the shadow of the backlit, life-sized statue of the school's founder.

Possum saw Denise entering through the left side of the twelve-foot oak doors. How innocent she looked. "Denise," he called, "over here." She squinted toward the sound of his voice.

"Will?" she said. All his other students respectfully called him Mr. Possum.

"Yes. Over here. Behind the statue. I need to talk to you."

He had practiced word choice and phrasing. Now was the moment he'd been dreading. He guided Denise to the quietest corner of the foyer, next to a seven-foot corn plant and away from the flow of students arriving for the seven o'clock classes. He looked at her directly. The hot summer air seemed to press them together.

"Look, Denise. You have really made a contribution to the class."

"Oh, thank you," she interrupted. "That's so cool."

"Writing is sensitive business," he started again.

"Only when you let it all hang out."

"It's not particularly an issue of hanging out."

"You got to tell it like it is. Tell the truth."

He tasted the first sourness of defeat. How could this mundane woman with her formidable convictions force him to feel so hopeless?

"I did not mean that we should not tell the truth. It is a question of adjusting to the sensitivity of the writer."

"I know sensitivity. You teach us real good." She smiled. "It's all about no pain, no gain."

Was she mocking him with her stare of excessive interest? He worried someone might overhear. My God, how she made him flounder under this silly corn plant, as awkward as an armadillo in a swimming pool.

"Each creative composition is so personal it makes a writer vulnerable," he said.

She nodded in full agreement.

He decided to be direct. "I must ask you to be considerate of other class members in your comments."

She recoiled slightly, frowning. "Shutting me down?"

"No. Not 'shutting you down.' Just soften your comments."

She looked away. "You've had complaints, haven't you? Well, it's not fair for them to come down on me. They're not good writers."

"Just go a little easier on the approach."

"It's the men, isn't?" she asked.

Possum swallowed. "No. It's not just the men!"

Discrimination, he wondered? Was she thinking of filing a complaint? His tongue stuck to the dry roof of his mouth. Where was his carefully planned congenial discourse that would lead to an open exchange of ideas on common ground?

"I wish you . . . I mean we . . . " she seemed uncomfortable with her thought.

"Just try. Okay?"

Without a word she hustled away, the strap of her large carryall swaddled in the cleavage of her breasts. There were still ten minutes before class. She did not go up the spiral staircase that led to the classroom. She went to the rest room. She closed the door without looking at him. Even though to see him, she would have had to move her head in a breakneck quick twist to the right, he saw significance in the fact that she didn't look.

He worried their talk had been too short. He had wished for the slightest apology. And why go to the rest room? To relieve herself? She'd just arrived! Or had she been devastated? Of course not! Not Denise. And he had been extremely gentle. But he pictured her in an emotional crisis, huddled in a stall with the sliding metal bolt on the door in the locked position.

In the classroom, Possum chatted with the other students and waited a few extra minutes beyond the hour for Denise to return. Finally he began without her. Ten minutes after class started, she entered. She was transformed—proud, demure, vulnerable, injured. She walked erect around the table to her chair holding her carryall and note pad until all the students' gazes were on her. No one spoke. Her lids were swollen. Her eyes rippled with the pinkness of a good cry. Her sweeping gaze of the room locked on Possum, unyielding. *My pain caused by him*, she did not need to say aloud. William Possum, cruel Associate Professor of English.

Possum got the class going again. Denise sat motionless and silent as the first two students read. The discussions were lively and informative. Possum relaxed a little. He may have lost a skirmish, but he felt he had won the war. Everyone, even Denise, had benefited. And Possum refused to worry about Denise's psyche. Denise was resilient. Even if in learning about herself she had been hurt a little, which Possum doubted, it wasn't as if she were going out to hang herself from a telephone pole. Maybe Alice Cherry had given him valuable advice.

Possum placed Denise's work on the bottom of the stack and silently prayed she would pass her turn to read. Her writing was terrible without exception. She had no concept of revision; a first write was a final product for her. She presented fragments of ideas that were totally unrelated as a finished story.

She loved to describe her work as spontaneous, insisting a lack of continuity among ideas was avant-garde. When asked what an incomprehensible paragraph meant, she said it was a "stream of consciousness," and she believed it jacked up the reader's need to discover his own creativity. She simply ignored constructive criticism or argued the critic couldn't understand. In essence, critics were stupid.

But even worse, her tidbits about humanity were crude and offensive. She was fond of dildos, intercourse in impossible positions, snuff sex and the like. Dreadful, Possum thought. When she read her work, the class sank into a silence of the tomb.

After two hours, he came to the last manuscript for the evening. "Denise. Would you like to read?"

"Oh, yes."

Possum struggled to find some theme in her 4000-word manuscript. Incestuous longings acted out in amazing detail.

Possum interrupted before Denise finished. "Time's up." He thanked Denise for her contribution.

"Hey. I'll finish next class," she said.

Possum blamed himself. His inability to control Denise exposed his lack of teaching proficiency, and Denise had become a turning point in his career. He believed a full professor could handle Denise. She demanded both experience and the professorial talent that led to promotions. She was one of the difficult challenges that everyone must meet on life's road to a full professorship, and he refused to let her defeat him. He didn't cherish another conference with Alice Cherry, but he saw political advantage to keeping her involved. So he reluctantly asked her again for help.

"Maybe you need to explore the dynamics of your students," Cherry said.

"Dynamics?" Why did Cherry, a chairperson, give him such vague instructions?

"What makes them tick. Why you react as you do."

"Where do I do that?"

"Look to a professional. Someone with insight. Roger Ownings, maybe."

So Possum invited Roger Ownings, the sociology teacher, for a beer and pizza at the local university pub. Roger was a long-time acquaintance and a man-about-town. "I've got a few things to talk about," Possum had said.

"I must say," Roger said after listening to Possum's overview of the problem, "you seem fascinated by this Denise."

Possum blushed and wished he had gone to a psychologist or a psychiatrist, although that would have required a two-hour drive to a bigger town. Clearly, Roger was untrained in these matters. And Cherry didn't know Roger lusted after every good-looking female student in his classes. Thoroughly unprofessional. But Possum must do what Cherry required, so he told Roger the details of how Denise managed to humiliate and anger his students.

Roger listened. "You have a like for her, William. I can hear it."

Possum suppressed his need to damn Roger's advice. Try to see his point! he thought. But Roger was wrong.

"I do not have a like for her," Possum said. "She ignores her lack of talent with total belief in her superiority. She has never taken one suggestion for improvement in her writing. She's really irritating."

"Well said, Possum. You're crazy for her."

"Stop it." Possum wished he could leave gracefully. He had never realized how much he disliked Roger. "She has this cocky attitude. The worst I've ever seen," he said.

"Correct me if I'm wrong," said Roger. "I bet she's young, well built, smiles widely with good teeth."

"She's overweight. She has absolutely no class. And she grins!" Denise loved to wear jean skirts to class, her soft flesh bulged over her waistband like bread dough expanding over the edge of a baking pan. Her form fitting shirts displayed overripe breasts spilling over the limits of a bra that struggled to contain them. Her nipples were always visible through the sheer elastic fabric, and their erectile activity, Possum believed, was positive proof of her unchecked passion. He was chained to wonder when they would pop out again with determination and suggestion, flooding him with embarrassment he could not suppress.

"What does she say?" Roger asked.

"She crucifies the language," Possum said in his lecturing tone. "Uses the "f" word whenever she wants. And she is full of misinterpretations. She believes men who say "hello" really mean, "Hi, let's procreate."

"Let yourself go," Roger said. "It's fuck, William, not procreate."

Possum sipped his beer, the liquid, bubbleless surface rippling from his tremor of anger. Roger refused to understand that Denise was destroying his career.

"Why don't you just date her? Tell her to quit coming to class so you can have a legitimate friendship," Roger said.

Possum leaned back aghast. "That's the worst advice. I can't date students. She's ten years younger. I'm up for promotion."

"She's not a real student. Not an undergraduate. This is adult education. Noncredit."

"I'm not attracted to students," Possum insisted.

"You could get to know her outside of class. You don't have to marry her."

"She's not my type."

"It might be worth a try. You're our most eligible bachelor."

"You're way off here, Roger. Way off."

They sipped their beers in silence. A tune on the jukebox started and finished.

"Great looking babes don't have problems in sociology. We get the unfortunate uglies with no appeal."

"You haven't listened to a word I've said."

"Got to go, my man. But listen to old Roger. Give her a chance."

"Roger," Possum said, "everything is not about sex."

"You're wrong, William. Without sex the sun would never rise."

The next day, Alice Cherry called an emergency meeting. An adult student, Maybelle Rather, had come to discuss Possum's teaching skills, and Cherry wanted Possum there.

Maybelle Rather, who matriculated under the senior citizen's discount rate, sat in Cherry's office, her back as straight as a ruler. "I can't stand anymore of her acid comments. Your class is a shambles,

Mr. Possum; there is no organization. You return our stories two weeks late. And you refuse to curb that Denise person. She is beyond human courtesy. I don't see how you can let her go on."

Possum shuddered. "Please don't give up," he urged. "I'll talk to her again. See if I can't get her to temper her approach."

Maybelle looked in doubt.

"Learning should be fun," Cherry said vaguely, but Possum could tell she was angry.

"There is no enjoyment when that woman is around. And she never misses a class!" Maybelle closed the door with a firm hand, and Alice Cherry turned to Possum.

"Why can't you solve these student problems?"

"I talked to Denise." He told her how it worked for most of one session. But that by the next session, she was right back to her insulting ways.

"What about Roger Ownings?"

Possum nodded. "He thought I should set up private meetings. Tutorials." He felt a twinge of guilt at his euphemism for Roger's suggestion of a date. "As an alternative to coming to class."

"Do it here in the department during the day. And keep me informed."

"Could someone else do it? Elsie or Harold?"

"You do it, William. You teach creative writing."

Denise was ecstatic about personal tutoring. Possum had been careful on the phone. He told her the class had continued to complain and, to please everyone, he thought that he should arrange special teaching sessions for her. He didn't fully agree with the class assessment, he said, but it seemed practical and, in addition, he could give her intensified instruction to help her writing. She agreed for sessions at 11:00 AM on Wednesdays.

She came dressed in a demure, white sleeveless dress and white flats. Her legs were bare and her skin glowed with perspiration. She had tied her hair back with a red ribbon. Possum thought the effect was a little childish and gave her the air of a farmyard maid.

"I think this is going to work out fine," Possum said.

"I want to write something really great."

"You're coming right along."

"The class is doing super. I mean, after our little talk and all. They're getting better."

"It's your education that is important to me," Possum said.

"You know, Will. You're a great teacher. You have what I like. With you everything is so . . . so big." She laughed.

Possum smiled through his apprehension of her crass double-entendres. "Thanks. I think I know what you mean."

"Why did you say that? 'You think you know what I mean.'"

"I wasn't sure about the 'big' idea." He smiled weakly.

She moaned. It was as if he'd rubbed a brass vessel and some hostile genie had emerged in a vapor cloud. She pouted. She put on a petulant ingénue sort of look. "I know I'm not polished. No one knows what it's like."

"You're . . ."

"It's like I'm talking to stones or something."

"You do just fine," he said, but he feared to encourage her too much.

She looked on the verge of genuine tears. Suddenly Possum felt his resistance collapsing.

"That's pure shit," she said.

"No, Denise. You're making progress."

"The class zeros out. Whacko. They think I'm some fucking freak."

Possum handed her a Kleenex from his desk drawer. A few large tears rolled down the edge of her cheeks. Now he felt responsible for her pain.

"Why don't you read now," he said.

"You really want it?" she sniveled.

"Yes," he said. "Read to me."

She crossed her legs and her skirt slipped up her thigh. Slowly and deliberately she began to pulsate the free foot up and down.

"Read it all the way through. As we do in class."

She read, holding the manuscript in front of her and occasionally glancing over at Possum, who sat rigidly.

She had written a set of loosely connected scenes for the session. As she read, Possum took notes on a yellow lined legal pad. He dared not interrupt.

After twenty minutes she stopped abruptly. With her never-ending sewer of sexual exploits, Possum wasn't sure whether she had finished.

"It's good?" she asked after a long pause.

Possum swallowed and stared out the window for a second. "I like the character . . ."

"Buster?"

"No. The third one. Evan."

"You mean Sean."

"Yes, Sean. But I did think the rape of a nine-year-old was jarring. I didn't see his motivation. If it were my story, I'd make the rape victim older and not so empty, change it so it's not an act of random violence."

"But Will, men are brutal. It's universal, like you're always talking about."

"I believe it's important to use universal themes. But the good story shows a character by a logical progression of acts and thoughts." He prayed she might be receptive to instruction.

"He had a thought. He wanted to ram it too her."

Possum shifted, the chair seemed too small for him.

"Maybe the victim could be flushed out a little too. More detail and something about her feelings."

"She's a victim. Not a perp."

He felt he was on a steeply sloped tin roof in the rain and his rubber-soled shoes were slipping. "Well, enhancing the reader's knowledge about characters can make their victimization even more dramatic."

"You think this is all shit, don't you?"

"Not at all," Possum said quickly.

"Don't lie, Will. The class said the same thing. It's all just shit."

"You have a wonderful gift for detail."

"Don't dig for something good."

"You shouldn't feel down. Every writer has self doubt."

"Why don't you just shove it up your ass."

"Denise, I didn't mean . . ."

"I'm tired of fucking flat heads telling me what's good and what isn't."

"Please, Denise . . ."

"Fuck you." She was flushed. She picked up her manuscript that had fallen to the floor. Possum tried to help but she pushed him away.

"Denise . . ."

"I trusted you. You twerp."

She put her mechanical pencil in her purse, extended her middle finger, and stalked out.

"Please, Denise . . ."

That evening, it took Possum until bedtime to calm down. He analyzed every detail of the session as if he were searching through his office jar of mixed jellybeans for those with the red cherry flavor. But he could not find where he went wrong.

The next day he didn't hear from Denise, and each hour he agonized over his responsibility. Should he try to contact her? He decided not. She was too unreasonable.

Denise did not show at the four Wednesday sessions she was entitled to. He waited the entire hour each time. She didn't call. Possum saw no success in teaching at their last meeting, but he felt he had achieved a resolution to her disruptive class habits. Not a crisp resolution. But at least final.

He told Alice Cherry that Denise had dropped out. His creative writing class emerged into less chaos, as if the students savored the contrast of their tranquil Denise-deficient sessions. Then, the summer session was finally over.

Three weeks later, Alice Cherry called Possum to her office. "I don't like to have to tell you this, but your promotion was turned down by the committee."

Possum thought he'd been prepared for it, but the reality turned his interior into a vacuum. It was seconds before he could reply.

"Did that creative writing class thing have anything to do with it?"

"No. Not just that. All your evaluations are terrible. I get complaints about your classes raging out of control. Your publications are non-existent. I don't think you'll ever make it."

Cherry's attack was too strong. She must have some other reason for not supporting him. "I'll never give up," he said forcefully.

"And William . . ."

"Yes . . ."

"Here is a list of the registrants for the upcoming creative writing class." She handed a sheet with a column of names. "Get a grip on this one, okay?"

Now he was thinking Denise had sunk him. She was a teacher's worst nightmare.

Possum scanned the list, numb with the reality of his failure. Seventeen students. Alphabetically listed. His gaze froze at the very bottom, stuck on the name—"Witherspoon, Denise." My God!

Of course he was not totally surprised. She always signed up for everything. But how odd he felt, and he turned his head quickly away from Cherry. With his eyes closed, he searched the absurdity of this sea of dread that Denise's name brought on. And over that vast expanse soared an albatross of expectation. He could not deny it; he was glad Denise was coming back.

He looked at Cherry who stared at him relentlessly. She had seen his albatross before. Would she ever let him be a professor of English?

"Do you want that Denise person in your class?" Cherry asked.

He considered his response carefully. "I can handle her," he said.

CURSE OF A LONELY HEART

In college, I had been attracted to my roommate, Peter Townsend. But after fifteen years of marriage to Amanda, my thoughts of Peter had faded, until I heard a rumor that he would interview for Chairman of the Department of Psychiatry at the University where I was a professor of botany. I called to invite him to our house for a dinner while he was in town. I told Amanda.

"Goddamn it, Tony. I don't like him."

"You could try," I said. There were a few minutes at my twentieth college reunion when I thought Amanda could never get enough of Peter.

"You made a move. He turned you down," I said.

"I've never 'made a move' on any man."

"That's a little disingenuous," I said. I was surprised at my anger. We had so little between us. And I truly didn't care if she slept with every man she met, as long as she was confidential.

"Only if you grill. We can eat outside," Amanda said.

"Do a sit-down dinner," I said. Amanda was a proud cook of exacting proportions, frequently adjusted temperatures, and rigid freshness. Peter deserved the best.

She finally agreed and insisted we invite another faculty couple, Ester (in social science) and Henry (in molecular biology), and Amanda's sister Madeleine, who was to balance the table as Peter's dinner partner. Madeleine was in library science, thirty-five years old and never married. She was attractive but with a porcelain-figurine look to her face and a frightened-rabbit personality that I did not think was Peter's taste. But I said nothing to Amanda.

We gathered together on a Thursday night. I had insisted that Peter be presented as the honored guest, and he fit easily into the role as if he expected nothing less. The dinner was below Amanda's usual standards for excellence—she complained she lacked time during the week—and she glared frequently at Peter as if her failures were his fault.

Ester started the dinner conversation. "Why would you be interested in a chair here?" she said.

"Opportunity," Peter said.

"Not to improve negotiations at home? That's how you medical doctors squeeze those high clinical salaries, isn't it?"

"Peter is not that kind of faculty," I said.

"How would you know, Tony? The department here is close to broke. The previous chair left under a cloud of harassment accusations."

"The department has an excellent reputation," I said.

Amanda came in from the kitchen wearing oven mitts and carrying a hot ceramic dish filled with a bubbling parsnip puree.

"Are you considering other positions?" Amanda asked Peter.

"As they come up," Peter said.

For the next two courses the conversation came in spurts and we drank wine in the silences. But just before dessert, Madeline told a story about her schnauzer falling into the bathtub, and Ester expressed concern about the poor quality of students applying for admission this year. Even Amanda seemed warmed to chatty—at least a little—and told of her recent trip to the Bahamas with her boss, the university Chancellor, for a conference. Henry, silent throughout with his own thoughts, finally said yes when asked if he wanted another piece of flourless chocolate cake.

After dinner we straggled to the living room. I directed Peter to our most comfortable overstuffed chair. Amanda, Madeleine and I sat in side chairs, and Ester and Henry took the sofa near the fire, seating that honored Peter at the heart of a half circle. Two open bottles of red wine were on the coffee table, and there was a plate of marzipan that Amanda had beaten and molded into bananas, grapes and lemons. A shaded floor lamp in the corner and the flames from the log fire gave us a low intensity but pleasing light. We were all smiling.

"I can't believe you're not married," murmured Ester to Peter, swaying on the sofa as if in a lifeboat, her cheeks flushed. In the last hour she'd stared at Peter continuously, ignoring Henry. Peter rarely looked at her.

"Are you gay?" Ester finally asked Peter.

Peter turned his head and stared. "Not that I've yet realized," he finally said good-naturedly. In college, nude, he had been a dream of a man. I remembered after a shower, water running over his defined figure, his abdominal muscles without a trace of fat. He was still a man's man.

"You're attracted to men but never act?" Ester persisted. She was a woman who clung to girlish guile as she approached middle age.

"Not at all," said Peter

"Every man has gay thoughts," Amanda said.

Her authoritative tone irritated me, and I glared at her to be quiet. "Not true," I said—I was sure Peter's thoughts were heterosexual. Amanda and I often disagreed in our unusual times of discussion. For the most part, we spent our time in the house in separate rooms. We had settled into a marriage with rare intimacy, and I had a circle of friends she didn't ask about.

"What do you think, Peter?" Amanda asked. "Every man has a touch of gay?"

I could tell the teasing about masculinity had begun to irritate Peter, and he was trying not to show it.

"I know the pain of love lost," Peter said. "I will never marry again."

"Undoubtedly with gay thoughts," Ester said. Her probing had been a flirt that fell flat. Peter seemed unaware.

"A woman trifled with my affections," Peter said. "I have not recovered."

"It's so easy to blame it on the woman," Amanda said.

"She made mistakes," Peter said, "but I never blamed her."

"Oh, that is so male. *She* made the mistakes!" Ester said.

"Don't presume what you don't know," Peter said.

"Tell us the details. Let us decide about love and affection," Amanda said.

"What man knows the meaning of love?" Ester said.

"I want to hear," Madeleine said.

Henry looked interested too. He was the kind of guy who would fantasize himself in freeze-frame poses with Peter's woman.

"Well, let me take a break and I'll tell you," Peter said. He went up the stairs to the second floor bathroom while we huddled around the wine.

"That was rude," Madeleine whispered to Amanda. Amanda could not suppress a dreamy adolescent gaze when looking at Peter.

"Grow up, Maddie," Amanda said. "He's a monster."

"I think he's a good guy," Henry said.

"Shut up, Henry," Ester said. "He's a fucking sexist."

Henry stared at the fingers of his right hand that he splayed for no reason. He'd repeated the gesture frequently since we'd left the dining room. "That's not fair, honey."

"You've got a rock for a brain," Ester said. She filled her wine glass.

"Look," I said, "Peter is our guest. It's not fair to put him on the spot."

"Loosen up, Tony," Ester replied.

Peter came down the stairs and sat again near the center point of our half circle, sinking down in the soft chair. Everyone could see he was eager to tell his tale.

He began . . .

※

The third year after I was appointed full professor in psychiatry, a medical school student, I'll call her Cathy, came to do research. Her project was clinical fluff, some idea that hypnosis at age regression levels could be used to pinpoint triggers of recurrent depression. Cathy saw patients in all faculty practices, but she spent more time with me than anyone else. Looking back on it, there was probably an unrecognized attraction from the very beginning. I found her competent and always available, and was careful to treat her no better or worse than any other student.

She was a small girl with light brown hair, a round face with slightly pinched features, and penetrating pale blue eyes. Her lopsided smile, more right than left— quickly became endearing—one of her best features. She was a runner with a svelte figure and dressed in professional silk blouses and colorful skirts with provocative hemlines.

As was routine after students completed a service rotation, she was invited to the annual department outdoor barbecue. In a social setting, I found her animated intelligence charming, and since she was technically no longer a student, I asked her for a date. She asked about my divorce—I'd been a bachelor for fourteen years, and she thought my maturity attractive.

In a few weeks we couldn't bear to be away from each other. It was a mutual attraction of a lifetime. At the end of internship, she accepted a pediatric residency in New Haven. I, of course, could not move from my position at the University in D.C., and we vowed to spend every weekend together until she could finish her two years of training. As it turned out, she could rarely leave her clinical responsibilities, and I traveled to her. In the second year, our weekends together became more infrequent. I would arrive ungreeted at the airport and take a taxi to sit alone in her cramped apartment on a bone crunching futon. When she finally left the hospital, she was too exhausted to make love.

In two years she managed only two trips to Washington, but I did take her to New York or Boston a few times. She began to talk of a formal wedding. In public, she referred to us as engaged and wore a plain gold ring when we went out that disappeared by the time we settled back in our hotel room.

But in truth, there were times when I felt like a stranger. My lifelong policy had always been honesty, and I told Cathy of the strain of traveling so far for so few unpredictable hours of watching her sleep. And I always added—repeatedly—how much I needed her. We can work it out, she said.

Just before we broke up, it was late autumn and the leaves were off the trees. The only flight available for the weekend made two stops and was two hours late. It was past eleven when we got to her apartment complex.

Cathy slowed in the lot with reserved parking. A van with dark tinted-windows crowded into her space between two smaller cars.

She parked on the street and I rolled my suitcase to the apartment and carried it up three fights of stairs. I went to shower. Cathy slipped into a tee shirt and shorts and turned to making her dinner. I had eaten during a layover.

She made a sandwich for herself and was eating at the metal-topped kitchen table when I sat across from her in my underwear to have a glass of wine. We heard a knock on the door, and Cathy put down her sandwich.

"Don't answer it," Cathy whispered, signaling me to be quiet.

A man's hoarse voice called her name, and the knocking got faster and louder.

I got my pants from the closet and fumbled in my hurry to get them on.

"Go away," Cathy called out.

The man began pounding the door.

"Cathy!" he yelled. The pounding increased.

"He'll go away," she said softly.

She seemed to be right. Footsteps retreated down the wooden floors of the hallway. She released her grip on my arm and I led her into the living room. She collapsed into an overstuffed chair, her limbs shaking.

I sat on the sofa opposite to her. My breathing began to slow.

"You know him?" I asked.

"I've seen him once," she said.

I was about to ask for details when the two hooked prongs of a tire iron splintered through the upper panel of the door. My gaze locked on hers in disbelief.

"Caaa—-thy," the attacker moaned. Then after another blow, "I know he's in there."

"Go away," Cathy said. "I'll call the police." But her last few words were buried in a crash of iron on wood.

Cathy turned off the floor lamp in the living room, as if a dim light might slow him down.

"Get knives," I whispered as we backed into the kitchen. She opened drawers and found a bread knife the length of a rat; she pointed to a small paring knife for me that would have been useless. Cathy's look had shifted from scared to terrified.

We retreated to the bedroom; the explosive sounds followed. Whap, groan, whap, whap. I wondered if the attacker had a gun.

"He's going to kill us," I said.

"Dear God," she said. I locked the bedroom door, twisting the pouty-lip dime-sized center circle in the handle.

Cathy cowered on the bed, her knifepoint straight up. I searched in her closet for a gun, or an axe, or even a ski pole. I came up with a metal clothes hanger and unwound the wire; maybe I could blind him.

The pounding got faster again. Cathy dialed 911 on the bedside phone. "We're being attacked," she screamed. She had to repeat the address twice. I wedged the back of a chair under the bedroom door handle and pulled Cathy off the bed and as far away from the door as possible. We crouched, weapons ready.

The attacker crashed into the apartment, bumping against the living room furniture. He started with his tire iron on the bedroom door; Cathy was wheezing. In less than a minute, he was through the door, shoving the chair barrier aside easily with one arm. I couldn't see his face in the dark.

"Get in the bathroom," I yelled to Cathy.

We clambered to the bathroom—no bigger than a hall closet. I flipped the light switch as Cathy climbed over the toilet into the tub so I could get the door closed. I pushed the center lock-pin in the door handle. The attacker's tire iron splintered the door panel and came within inches of my face. I stumbled, knocking Cathy down.

The attacker kicked out the door panel and reached in and twisted the door handle from the inside. When the door opened, he froze and stared first at me and then at Cathy. He was almost six feet tall with narrow shoulders and a beginning potbelly. He looked about thirty. He wore glasses, a tee shirt and tan cotton pants. His scruffy running shoes had untied laces, and he wore a wide belt that held an automatic pistol.

Cathy had one leg over the edge of the tub; he stared at her thigh. She pointed the knife at him, twisting the shower curtain to cover herself. I gripped the showerhead with one hand and waved my clothes hanger.

He rested the curve of his tire iron on the bathroom tiles and we had a few seconds to think. He was now strangely subdued.

"So this is the boyfriend?" he said, looking to me as if I were some inferior cut of beef just served in an overpriced restaurant.

"Fiancé," said Cathy.

"I should kill him," the attacker said. His voice was breathy and mean.

He backed into the bedroom pointing the pistol at me with his right hand and holding the tire iron with his left. Cathy sobbed. "Get out," she said. Then, this guy, whose name turned out to be Kyle, sat on the bed and wept, moaning.

I let out a giddy laugh when I realized I wouldn't die. Cathy walked to the bed and tried to take the gun from Kyle, who pushed her away.

Two cops arrived and asked questions to Cathy and Kyle—because of their youth—as if they were betrothed and I were the stranger. I tried to maintain a dignity, but I was fighting humiliation at being ignored as some elderly nobody.

After ten minutes the man cop arrested Kyle taking him to the station and the woman cop stayed behind to write the formal report. I pretended disinterest.

Cathy told her story. She had met Kyle on a rare night off when she was lonely and went to a party for singles. They talked for a few minutes. "You're everything I ever wanted in a woman," Kyle had said. At that point, she told him she was engaged and to leave her alone. After the party Kyle became more determined, and he started calling her five, six times a day. As the cop finished writing, I stared a Cathy in disbelief. Why hadn't she been honest enough to tell me? The cop finally left.

The door to the apartment was useless. Cathy found a sheet, and by using lots of thumbtacks, we covered the holes in the door. Then I backed the sofa and tilted it on end so that it blocked most of the opening.

We got in bed and propped pillows against the headboard. We sat in silence.

"Who really is this Kyle?" I finally asked. She was still breathing fast. He was a computer programmer whose hobby was making kites in the shapes of dragons, snakes and carnivorous dinosaurs. That was all she knew.

"You dated?" I asked.

"Never," she said. "I didn't lie. He was at one party."

Despite her denial, the thought of Kyle and Cathy as a couple overwhelmed me. Women went to singles parties to pick up guys, right? I sulked.

"Forget him. I've wanted to see you so much," she said.

"Look. I'm angry. Okay? I mean, I come to visit my fiancée, and her boyfriend tears down the door and wants to kill me."

"He *isn't* my boyfriend. Can't you just hold me?" she said.

I flushed. "I didn't diddle with other girls."

She began crying.

"Did you screw?" I asked.

"What a terrible thing to say," interrupted Amanda.

"Chauvinist. You hadn't even committed," Ester said.

"What did she say?" I asked.

She said: "Of course not." She turned away from me. And we fell into silence.

The electric clock on the night table had an irritating drone and a click as the second hand staggered around the iridescent dial. I kept at least eighteen inches between us.

I stayed silent, my breathing strained. I listened to the night-sounds of the normal people living around us. Bath water running. A toilet flush. A yell in the parking lot. A car starting up. I felt as if I didn't belong.

At one point she touched me gently on the side of my face and I moved farther away. At six thirty, first light slipped into the room under the window shade. Cathy got up to make coffee.

In the daylight, the sofa propped on end against the door looked ridiculous, and the sheet we had tacked up barely covered the opening and was so transparent I could see the apartment door across the hall.

I told Cathy I would leave that afternoon. A day early.

"I'm afraid," she said. "I can't get the door fixed until Monday."

Without a word, I went out back to a trash heap behind the complex and picked out a set of mismatched boards. Then, using some nails I found in her utility closet and with a rock I retrieved from the edge of the parking lot, I nailed a barrier over the door, board-by-board, inch-by-inch. She could go in and out through the window to the iron fire escape.

"Can't you just love me?" she asked.

I had no conversation in me. I turned away and quickly packed. When I left for the airport by taxi, Cathy stayed in the bedroom behind the closed door.

Years later, she married a doctor.

I never saw her again.

⚭

We sat in silence for a while. Amanda was the first to speak.

"You should have believed her. She loved you."

"She should have told me about Kyle," Peter said. "She had some deep-seated reason for not telling me. It was a matter of trust."

"Why don't you look into yourself for all that deep-seated crap," Ester said. "You rejected her. You ought to be jailed." Ester threw a closed fist into the air.

"You were a jerk," Amanda said.

"She sacrificed so much for you," Ester said, her voice rippling in anger. "This Cathy. She's a saint."

"I'll agree she wasn't evil," said Peter. "But she made a mistake going to that party, and she couldn't admit to it."

"There is nothing more precious than a woman's love," Madeleine said softly.

Henry looked up in disgust to where the ceiling met the wall. Ester squeezed her lids shut to avoid looking at Madeleine whose moist eyes glinted in sympathy for Peter.

"Don't tell us you never dated other women," Ester said. "All those years."

"My only liaisons were necessities of my profession. They were hardly dates."

"You're unbelievable," Amanda said.

Peter flushed. He stood and walked to the door. I stood to dissuade him, but Amanda pulled me back down and shushed me. The silence was hostile. Peter said nothing, putting on his coat and closing the front door without looking back.

I looked around. Everyone, except Madeline, seemed relieved he was gone.

"We should have been a little more gracious to him," Madeleine said to Amanda. "He has so much more depth than I imagined."

"He's an asshole," Amanda said

"I thought him sensitive," I said.

Ester put her glass on the coffee table with a thud. "That's what I've never liked about you, Tony," she said. "The way you treat women."

Amanda laughed.

"Don't turn on me," I said. "Peter's a good friend. He was right to question that girl's feelings for him."

"What he did to the girl was inexcusable," Ester said. Madeleine frowned.

"She made the choice. He was the one always going to her. He sacrificed." My voice was loud. "No one should tolerate her deceit."

"You're obnoxious, Tony," Ester said. "I've always thought that. I'm glad the wine let me say it."

"Is that what you think?" I asked Amanda. "I'm out of line here?"

She paused. "You're wrong, Tony," she said.

I stood. I would not be insulted in my own home. I climbed the stairs and shut the door to my room. I stood in the dark, listening as the guests argued for a while, then said their goodbyes. I took off my clothes without turning on the light and left them rumpled on a chair. I went to bed in my underwear and stared at the ceiling.

An hour later, Amanda opened the door to my room. She sat down gingerly on the edge of my single bed near the foot and looked to the dark window. She was quiet for many minutes.

"We're sad, you and I," she finally said.

"Speak for yourself," I said. I wondered at the sincerity of her coming to me like this. She was very close to my leg. There was a blanket between us, but I could feel her presence. She laid the palm of her hand above my knee, her fingers spread slightly apart, but when I didn't respond she took it away. I could see only the indistinct outline of the side of her face in the dark. I stayed quiet.

After a few more minutes, she left. She closed the door with extended gentleness so no sound was made.

Sleep had still not come when the morning light seeped through the window under the shade. The bed covers had slipped off. I was still on my back, my hands on my chest with fingers interlaced, my feet touching. I was alone.

SUCHIN'S ESCAPE

Antoine lit a cigarette with the lighter from the dash of the twenty-seven year-old 1976 Lincoln Continental and leaned forward with both forearms on the steering wheel. Harry beat out a rhythm on the dash with both hands—BOOM chee CHEE—*di di* BOOM; and he sang a song of lost love. Antoine liked the tune, liked the way his cousin could make it flow.

Antoine watched the green two-story frame house across the street from where they were parked on a side street in Gretna. The image of the thin child Suchin, the eleven year old Chinese girl, materialized in the dark narrow alley between the houses, the blurred outline of a man blocking the alley behind her. She was naked except for a pair of patent leather Mary Janes. She stopped before stepping into the glint of the morning sun, and slid a lace trimmed white dress over her head, pushing her arms out the sleeve holes. She smoothed the fabric in front with both hands and the hem fell to her ankles.

"She's done," Antoine said. Harry stopped his rhythm and got out of the car. He met the girl still in the shadows, grabbed her arm, and brought her quickly to the car, her moving feet barely touching the ground. Harry opened the back door and shoved her into the back seat.

"Don't push me." Suchin said, kicking out, her shoe heel glancing off Harry's arm.

The girl made money and this guy in the shadows was one of her many repeats. But Antoine didn't trust her. Something about the way her eyes held his, hard and cold in their darkness, and the way she never flinched if he had to cuff her.

"Tape her," he said. "I got a bad feeling."

"We ain't going that far," Harry said.

See! Even Harry was ornery now, started about the time this girl arrived in a shipment of twelve. Strange too, because the kid was all girl—not anything womanly—like a twig in a forest of leafy branches.

"That Paradise Motel near the airport," Antoine said.

"Tape hurt," said Suchin.

That proved it. Pure trouble . . . the way she'd just butt in like she belonged.

"Ride with her then," he said to Harry.

Harry shoved Suchin over to one side on the back seat to make room. He slammed the back door as Antoine cranked the motor.

"But don't put them locks down," Harry said.

Harry was a goddamn two year-old trapped in the body of King Kong sometimes. Antoine undid the childproof locks on the back doors.

"Don't like the door locked," Harry said, feeling foolish when the fear of being closed in grabbed him.

The Lincoln Continental rolled down the expressway. Antoine kept in the right lane, five miles an hour below the speed limit. Harry's big head blocked half his view out the rear view mirror. He checked the side mirrors for cops. He was clean, but Harry had a prior for assault with a parole violation.

The kid wasn't in the mirror. He glanced back over his right shoulder. Nothing. She was either lying down or she'd slipped over next to the door. He reached for a rumpled cigarette pack wedged between the windshield and the dash, squeezed out the end of the last cigarette that he extracted with tight lips, and lit up.

The silence from the back seat mounted.

Then the tap . . . tap . . . tap . . . tap. The kid was beating her shoe against the doorframe, grooving on the beat like a pro, the pulse asking for more. Sure enough, Harry's big hands clapped soft but firm with emphasis on the late off beats. Tap tap CLAP tap CLAP tap CLAP CLAP.

Without thinking Antoine beat his thumb against the steering wheel. He tucked the Lincoln in behind a bakery truck.

Harry started singing, his voice filling up the car, and the kid making ooou-ooous like a real backup.

"It's down" tap tap

"In Pascagoula" tap tap

"Where the women" tap tap

"Do the hoola" tap tap

"And the men" tap tap

"They the ones" tap tap.

"They the ones, whoooo———ooooooooooooo"

"Wicky . . . wicky . . . whacky—whacky—woo."

For a few bars Harry and Suchin clapped and tapped almost perfectly in their shared drive. Then they shifted in unison to a slower groove, four to the bar. Harry's voice fell off a minor third.

"Ohhhh, ohhhh," he wailed.

"Ouuuuu, ouuuuu" the kid chimed in,

"It's my woman," ... "ohhh, yeah,"

"That cheating woman," ....

"ouuu, ouuu,"

"It's my woman," "ohhh, yeah,"

"That done me wrong." Harry finished.

"Soooo wrong," the kid added. "Ouuuuu . . ."

Harry chuckled.

Then, smooth as a river running, the two of them were back working on and off the beat, setting up for another verse.

Goddamn her. She could work Harry like a dog jumping through hoops.

"Tolls," he said.

Harry shoved Suchin down in the foot well to hide her as Antoine held bills out to the collector. "Be quiet," he said.

The engine strained when the Lincoln started up the bridge incline over the Mississippi. Two minutes later the car slowed in traffic. Suchin stiffened, her teeth clenched.

She yanked the door handle, shoved the door open, rolled out headfirst flipping on her back. In seconds she was up running toward the guardrail, the river, so much bigger than the stream that ran near her village in China. Horns blared. Fast cars moved in the opposite direction. Harry yelled behind her. How close was he? A sports car hit her, throwing her up on the hood, screeching to a stop. The girders above her weaved like dragons' tails.

Harry grabbed her before she slid off to the pavement, held her so close his hot breath smothered her face. Her leg began to throb, she could barely see out one eye, but her heart squeezed fast and strong.

"Shouldn't done that," Harry whispered to her. "Antoine going to kill you."

The sports car guy came running up screaming about his innocence. With one arm still holding Suchin, Harry picked him up and threw him against the side of the car so hard his head flew back on the roll bar with a crunch. Harry grunted satisfaction as the guy slumped half conscious.

Suchin moaned when Harry put her in the car.

"Stay with her," Antoine said. He blew the horn, waved at people. He had to get moving before any cops came. He'd have to switch the plates again, find something in the Marriott parking garage from Ohio or Indiana this time. In a couple minutes they were at the exit ramp. He was out of cigarettes.

The kid trembled, her head in Harry's hands, her shoulders on his thigh, her legs out on the seat.

"She breathing?" Antoine asked into the back seat.

"Blood coming out her mouth." A trickle of dark red mixed with spit-foam dripped on Harry's thigh. "Her leg getting big," he said.

Antoine caught a red light. He looked back. The girl's chest moved with quick in and outs. Her dress was torn. Her upper leg a sick purple. No one would pay for sex with a bleeding, moaning kid. He hated to stiff the guy on Airline Highway but he headed for Claiborne to get on the I-10.

"She bad," Harry said. "She real bad."

Suchin heard Harry's words as if the volume had been turned to maximum in a set of headphones. She did not think about dying, and she wondered if she could run with her leg hurting.

She coughed.

"What was that?" Antoine said.

Harry saw a bloody tooth on the seat. "She bad," he repeated.

Well, shit. Antoine was going as fast as he could without putting them behind bars.

"Her eye look crooked," Harry said like he blamed Antoine.

It was Harry's fault she got out. No locks! Harry had jumped at the click of a deadbolt sliding home since he was in Angola for two years five months. Like he caught a phobia and now we can't lock the back doors.

Antoine wasn't being unreasonable. Okay. He didn't like kids. But he wasn't a monster. And he never let a guy down. Or a kid, for that matter. He was taking her to the doc, for Christ sake. How many guys would do that? "How many?" he said out loud.

"What you say?" Harry said.

But he didn't explain. Harry was slow to understand sometimes. And too soft to keep rules.

He pulled into in a mall and parked. Harry followed him carrying the kid through the door, between a liquor store and a Goodwill clothing outlet, marked in faded yellow letters:

OFFICE HOURS 10-2
M,W,Th

The doc sat alone at a desk in a single room. Harry laid Suchin on a bare examining table with metal stirrups on one end.

"That's repulsive," the doc said swiveling back and forth in his chair, his short-sleeved pale tan shirt with yellow brush-like swirl patterns unbuttoned halfway down the slope of his hairy chest. He was a hundred pounds overweight.

"Hit by a car."

"Take her to Charity."

"She's illegal."

"I don't do trauma."

Suchin's leg spasmed for a few seconds.

"The big man pays you damn good," Antoine said. "Too much."

"Not for this." The doc belched; Antoine was close enough to whiff the scent of decayed oranges and cheap booze—like the man's insides needed to be flushed down a toilet.

The doc stood up. He took a wooden tongue blade from his shirt pocket. He lifted the kid's dress fabric with the blade careful not to touch anything bloody. Still with the tongue blade, he pushed up a swollen eyelid and stared at a pupil.

"She'll live."

"Aren't you going to x-ray or something?"

"Do you see an x-ray machine?"

"She could die."

"She isn't going to die!" he said.

The doc picked up a wallet off his desk and left through a back door that went straight to a service alley. "Office is closed," he said as he slammed the door shut.

Antoine pointed for Harry to get the kid.

"Where we going?"

"Auntie's," Antoine said. "She'll do something."

Suchin felt the big arms cradling her again, her mind clear. Her stomach churned. Her tongue probed the sore little craters where her teeth were gone. Her leg ached but she thought she could walk if she had to. With her non-blurred eye she searched from habit for locks on the doors. Then, when the sunlight glared on her, she squeezed her good eye closed and went limp to let Harry think her mind had shut down her body for a while.

The Lincoln got to Auntie's in Plaquemine Parrish just before five, a rooster tail of almost white dust pluming up behind that monster car. Auntie went downstairs out of the farmhouse, stood there waiting as they drove up, her arms crossed. She was heavy, big boned, and barren; her blood Indian, Creole, and Black, and every corpuscle heavy with this love-hate feeling for kids. It was a mystery why she took care of them at all after being in the trade for thirty years.

"You whack this one?" Auntie said to Antoine as Harry worked at getting Suchin out of the car so she didn't hurt.

"Watch your mouth," Antoine said.

Auntie's hands probed Suchin's thigh while she was still in Harry's arms. Suchin cried out. She pushed on Suchin's belly. Suchin moaned. She looked under Suchin's swollen eyelid. Suchin's eye was seeing well now and she locked on Auntie's gaze. Auntie frowned and turned away.

"Put her to the right of the door in the bedroom," Auntie said to Harry and pulled Antoine's shirt to move him a few feet so no one could hear.

"Cash up front." she said.

"She's big money. Next to top in the convention trade. She good for it. We ain't got cash."

"Out of where?" Auntie asked.

"Mere Bull. In Kenner."

"Tell Mere Bull she to bring that cash down here personal."

"You got my word," Antoine said sincerely.

"Ain't that a lot of slippery shit?"

Suchin lay on her back on a cot with no mattress. The only window had a yellow shade pulled down and the dim light from the filtered sun wasn't strong enough to define the floral details on the scruffy wallpaper. Two bunk beds were stacked as a unit against the opposite wall. The lump of a girl bulged under a sheet, the ends of her straight long hair—shiny as a black, lacquered piano—hung over the edge of the lower bunk. The upper bunk didn't have a mattress.

Harry was gone, but his words stayed with Suchin. "Give it up," he said as his breath tickled her ear, "The beat don't work good." He didn't touch her.

Suchin dozed to the sounds of flies chasing each other around the room. She woke just before all the light faded. The girl under the sheet hadn't moved. Suchin could hear Auntie bumping around somewhere down below on the first floor.

Suchin was achy all over, but less now. Her leg throbbed but when she stood and pressed down, the pain eased a little.

"Who you?" she called to the lump on the bed.

She waited a minute. "You living?"

She hobbled over slowly and peeled back the sheet. She sucked in a rush of air.

"You beautiful," she said suddenly aware of trying to use her very best English. The girl had the delicate sculpted features of a porcelain doll and her eyes were wide open, the whites showing all around irises so brown they seemed almost as black as the pupil. She stared straight through Suchin, deep into some other galaxy.

"My name's Suchin. From China. Six months. Came on a ship."

The girl didn't change.

"You sleep like that?" Suchin asked. "Your eyes open?"

She thought the girl's eyes focused a little, her lips parted slightly.

"You like it here?"

The girl closed her eyes slowly, she was breathing faster, and she turned away. She wasn't a druggie, Suchin thought. Her eyes were too hard for that.

Auntie's mountainous form filled the open door behind Suchin. Auntie came into the room, light from the hall making a faint halo behind her.

"She talk to you?" Auntie asked.

Suchin didn't move keeping her back to Auntie.

"Well, don't you be bothering her," Auntie said. "She's having some time to herself until she talks again."

Suchin stayed stone still, not knowing how to feel about Auntie. But she wasn't afraid.

Auntie gave Suchin a bowl of red beans and rice with a plastic spoon stuck in it and pulled up a chair next to the girl to begin feeding her soup from a Campbell's can. "Mushroom only thing she'll eat. Don't like tomato," she said, mostly to herself.

When she finished Auntie turned to take Suchin's empty bowl. "You moving better than I thought. You scamming Auntie?"

Suchin stayed quiet.

"Well, you pick up that chamber potty and empty it in the bathroom down the hall before I lock up again. Wash it out good too."

For hours after Auntie closed the door and turned the key in the lock, Suchin lay on her cot; but no sleep came. She wondered where that girl's eyes were looking, what they saw. She wondered if she was thinking about the men. How men treated girls. She wondered if the girl thought too, if you did right, maybe someday a man take you away and be good to you. All the girls had heard of that happening—a nice man. But they never knew anyone it happened to, only knew by the story telling that skipped from girl to girl like a flu bug.

※

It was still half dark when Suchin woke. The lump girl was sitting on the floor cross-legged, her hands on her stomach and she was rocking slow—front, back, front.

Suchin eased off the bed and stretched, watching the girl. Suchin's leg and chest hurt less.

Two glasses of water and a saucer with two oven-cooked rolls sat on the floor inside the locked door. Suchin drank and ate a roll. "You want this?" she said tempted to eat the second roll. But the girl said nothing and Suchin left the water and the roll close enough for her to reach.

Suchin's leg didn't bend easily, and she lay down on her side, her legs straight out to one side, her head propped up on her hand with her arm on the floor bent at the elbow.

The black-haired girl rocked. Forward. Back. Forward.

"My mother's dead. Father dead too," Suchin said staring under the bed as if to find some hidden non-person in the dark recess.

Back, forward, back, the girl went on. Her eyes never blinking.

"Yours too? Your parents?"

Forward, back, forward, about as fast as a pendulum in a giant clock.

"It's okay. I know you're like the rest of us. Sometime you need to get away."

The girl still rocking.

The door unlocked and Auntie came in. "In the name of God, leave that child alone. You too healthy and she too sick for you to keep bothering her." She yanked Suchin up to sitting then grabbed the girl's shoulder to stop her rocking and held the glass of water to the girl's mouth. The girl swallowed a few times.

"Now for you," she said grabbing Suchin. "I'll take you to the bathroom to wash that dried blood off. Then I'll sew up that dress and give it a good wash."

That night after Auntie put them both in bed, Auntie came back in with a flashlight because the light socket for the screw-in bulb in the ceiling was empty. She sat in a chair next to the girl's bed, her back to Suchin. She opened a book with a torn red cover. Suchin was lying on her cot, looking to the ceiling.

"'It was Toto,'" Auntie read in a low singsong voice.

"Who was Toto?" Suchin asked.

"Shut your face," Auntie said shining the light straight into Suchin's eyes. "This is Helen's story."

Suchin turned away but not far enough so she couldn't hear.

"You don't need story telling," Auntie said to Suchin before turning her flashlight back to the book again to read.

"'It was Toto that made Dorothy laugh, and saved her from growing as gray as her other surroundings.'" Auntie paused. "'Toto was not gray; he was a little black dog, with long silky hair and small black eyes that twinkled merrily on either side of his funny, wee nose. Toto played all day long, and Dorothy played with him, and loved him dearly.'"

"Who's Dorothy?" Suchin couldn't keep from asking.

"She's an orphan. Now hold your tongue." But the meanness was not in her voice.

Auntie continued loud enough that Suchin could hear. "'Today, however, they were not playing. Uncle Henry sat upon the doorstep...'"

Suchin wondered what Uncle Henry would do to Dorothy, then listened all about Kansas and Oz, a world that, as Auntie continued reading, Suchin imagined might be the real America.

The lightning bolt lit up the room bright as day just after two AM. Suchin sat straight up and in the after-flash, the room seemed pitch black, even the thin strip of pale yellow under the door from the hall overhead bulb was wiped out. Suchin stood up, limped to the window, and raised the shade. The sky swirled with grey clouds; sheets of rain streaked across the yard and lightning pulsed the pewter sky.

The girl was sitting too, her eyes fixed on Suchin.

"It's okay," Suchin said, recovering quickly. She had survived too many nights in the open hut of her grandmother—or more recently the lean-to she shared with her uncle for a while—with storms raging around her—to worry. She sat next to the girl.

"We got to get away," Suchin said. "You understand?"

The girl stared at her with eyes black in the darkness. She turned her head and her black hair flowed around her face.

"Now!"

"No," the girl said. Her voice was deep and raspy.

"We can do it."

"No!" She shoved Suchin away and she took a deep breath and screamed.

"What are you doing?"

"You go!" the girl said.

"You too."

"I can't," she said. "I don't think right sometime."

The girl's eyes had shifted from terror to some fierce determination. She screamed again, getting off the bed and she took a chair that Auntie had been reading in and smashed the window twice so all the glass was gone.

The key in the lock turned and as Auntie rumbled in, the girl, after a quick glance of clear-bolt sanity thrown at Suchin, headed for the window, throwing herself half out, but not far enough to fall.

Auntie lunged across and grabbed the girl by the legs. "You crazy!" she said. "It's a long way down."

The door was open. Suchin slipped out, felt her way down the stairs, out the front door, across the porch. She could see orange groves outlined against the sky. Rain swept across her face until she reached the protection of the first line of trees. She stumbled on, running as fast as her sore leg would allow. It would be many minutes before Auntie could follow. She heard Helen still screaming, demanding Auntie's attention. Even hurting, Suchin knew she could keep her distance from someone as big and slow as Auntie. In minutes she reached the river and headed down stream looking for something that would float. Soon the rain stopped, the wind died, and an almost full moon threw glints on the surface of the water.

Antoine and Harry arrived the next morning to take Suchin back. Auntie didn't offer them anything to drink.

"Last I saw of her she was headed for the grove, toward the river. It was a hell of a storm."

"We got to take her away," said Harry.

"Jesus," said Antoine. "Did you go after her?"

"I don't go looking for runaways."

"Mere Bull transferred her to Houston," Antoine said. "They got tight discipline down there. And she's a money maker."

"That girl full of Tabasco."

"There's only one road out. That's where she'll be."

"She don't know the road or the river."

"You think she's hiding?"

"Maybe. But she's smart as they come. Might be long gone by now."

Antoine signaled Harry to move to the car. "Road's the only way out."

"Where's my money?" Auntie asked.

"I ain't paying for letting the kid get away," Antoine said.

Antoine was out the door, following Harry to the car.

Auntie grabbed her shotgun from behind the kitchen door. Stepped back outside.

"Cocksucker," Auntie yelled. She was waving the shotgun, holding it with one hand in the middle. "You ever show up here again, I'll blow your head off."

There was a white girl standing in the door behind Auntie. Even from a distance she was so ghostly beautiful with her white skin and long black hair glistening like black silk. One of the nut cases Auntie was famous for bringing back into the world for service. Antoine slammed the door and drove off.

"That Auntie's one weird bitch," he said to Harry. "Probably let the kid go."

⁓∞⁓

Antoine and Harry used up a tank of gas cruising the only long road that led out of the Parrish but they didn't see the girl.

"You think she all right?" Harry asked.

"She got to be alive or we're gator meat," Antoine said. "She's worth a lot of money."

Antoine had to poke Harry to keep him awake, keep him looking. You big dumb gorrilla, he thought. But Harry was good kin. Shit. They'd drawn women's tits on the bathroom walls at school together. They'd buddied up with whores. Harry had saved his life too, once on a B and E when the owner tried to kill him with a shotgun, once in a knife fight in the ninth ward.

At night they slept in the car in a truck stop parking lot before heading south in the early morning. They changed their search, asking in the towns for anyone who'd seen a pretty barefoot Chinese girl about four feet high wearing a ripped up white dress.

It was just after eleven o'clock they cornered Suchin in the storeroom of a convenience store just North of Venice. The woman owner had let a Chinese girl sleep for a few hours after her daughter found her down near the river and brought her home.

※

Suchin awoke startled by an outside noise. The windowless room was black until the door opened and light from the store's fluorescent overhead bulbs outlined Antoine's silhouette coming toward her. Framed in the door behind him was the bulk of Harry. Antoine gripped her arm, with the force she knew and dreaded, and pulled her upright. In seconds he'd dragged her into the store toward the high counter where the woman owner stood watching. Suchin looked around. Through the glass door on the front she could see two gas pumps with a red pickup truck parked in front with the tailgate down and long lengths of lumber sticking out a few feet with a red flag hanging limply on the end of the longest board. A door to the restroom opened. She watched a man come out, go through the door toward the pick up. Harry went into the restroom.

Antoine let her go and he turned to buy a lighter and cigarettes. She slipped down the isle between the motor oil and potato chips, out the door. She grabbed the lumber on the back of the truck and pulled her self up as the truck accelerated and lurched without a stop onto the road. She was in the truck and lying face down, the truck bed vibrating under her as it went through gears to reach cruising speed. She stayed low. Within two minutes, looking back, she saw the Lincoln, the headlights flashing. It gained on the truck, the horn blaring. The pickup slowed. Antoine pulled up to the side of the truck. He was yelling for the pickup to pull over. The pickup stopped. Antoine parked the Lincoln in front of the truck, off the road. Suchin slipped down from the truck bed and limped up a drive toward a house, but Antoine and Harry reached her before she could hide.

Harry was breathing hard.

"What a way to make a living," Antoine said as he and Harry took Suchin back toward the Lincoln.

The pick up truck driver was explaining he didn't know she was there.

"I'm cool," Antoine said.

"Why are you chasing her?"

"Wise up, man. Forget you ever saw her."

While Harry held Suchin, Antoine emptied the trunk of the Lincoln—a bag of golf clubs, a Styrofoam cooler, fishing rods, small outboard motor, and a five-gallon can of gasoline. He put them in the back seat. Then with two-inch tape he bound Suchin's arms to her chest with around-the-body passes from shoulders to waist. It was hard for Suchin to take a deep breath.

"I could keep her up front," Harry said.

Antoine lifted Suchin's dress and made seven passes of tape around her thighs. "I ain't taking any chances. We got a long way to go." He made seven more passes of tape around her ankles. She was still standing when he picked her up and put her in the trunk. "Damn if she can get out of that."

Harry held the trunk lid open when Antoine tried to close it.

Antoine wanted to belt Harry, but he held back. They needed to be moving. "Be sure it's locked," Antoine said and went to the front.

Harry turned Suchin on her back, took a loose tire iron out from under her and put it next to the back of the seat where it wouldn't hurt and shut the lid. In minutes they were on their way to Houston, back through New Orleans because that was the only way out of the delta.

Antoine smoked continuously as he drove. Harry slept with his head against the door until they reached Port Sulfur. Suchin had cried out a few times, but there were no sounds from the trunk now.

"Maybe she don't need to go to Houston," Harry said.

"And maybe Mere Bull and the big man will just be happy that all that money to get the kid bought in China on top of the cash to ship her and slip her in will never be returned."

"Houston not a good place."

"Maybe they send her back when she gets broken in," Antoine said.

"She got the beat."

"They're kids, for Christ sake. You got to learn not to care, Harry. They ain't like regular people."

They stayed quiet, passing through Algiers, then New Orleans, then up on the I-10. Soon they were near the airport.

Suchin was yelling.

"See if you can tell what she wants," Antoine said.

Harry leaned over the seat and pushed the motor and gas can aside. "She needs to pee."

"Shit. Tell her we ain't stopping till we get to Houston."

Harry told her loud so she could hear through the backseat.

"I got to go bad!" she yelled. Antoine heard that.

Harry came back in the front seat. "We got to let her pee."

"Okay. Okay!" Antoine pulled onto the breakdown lane where it was dark. He popped the trunk lid. "Go get her."

Antoine opened the front and rear doors on the right side. "Bring her in between the doors. No one will see."

Harry set her down on her feet between the doors and had to hold her upright; she was too tightly taped to bend.

"I can't sit," she said.

"Do it standing up then."

"I can't."

"We got to cut the tape," Harry said.

"We ain't cutting the tape. I've only got a couple feet left."

"Let it go," Antoine said to Suchin and hit her lightly on the head. Harry still held her, afraid she'd fall over.

"I can't." But in a few seconds her dress went dark, and then a puddle formed in the dust.

"I'm wet."

"That's so terrible," Antoine whined.

"We should have cut the tape," Harry said.

"Put her in the back. I ain't touching her."

"We got something to wipe her off?"

"Some paper towels under the seat."

They were back on the road. Harry rested against the door but didn't sleep. Antoine turned on the radio.

"What if she calls out or something?" Harry said.

"Won't make any difference."

"We won't hear!"

"Okay, I'll turn it down!" Antoine turned the music down a little.

Harry reached forward and turned it off.

"Hey, asshole. I'm not going all the way to Houston without music," Antoine said.

Traffic was light. Antoine drafted behind an eighteen-wheeler in the slow lane to avoid attention.

Suchin called out about half an hour later. "I can't breathe!"

"Did you hear that?"

"She must be breathing. She's yelling, for Christ's sake.'

"We got to check."

"We don't have to check. I'm not stopping until we need gas."

"There might be no air back there."

"There's enough."

Harry stared straight ahead for a few minutes. "She ain't said nothing," he said.

"We got an hour, Harry. An hour before we need gas!"

Harry growled as he turned to shove Antoine on the shoulder, shoving him up against the driver's-side door. "We got to check."

Antoine looked at Harry in surprise. "Jesus, Harry. Don't ever do that again. I'd have to whack you." He kept driving.

Harry was breathing fast, his eyes wide with anger. He drew back and threw a right fist at the side of Antoine's head. Antoine blacked out for a few seconds, his hands slipping off the wheel, the cruise control holding steady. The Lincoln left the road, Antoine alert in seconds, realized the danger, turned the wheel—jammed the brakes; the car swerved to the left and the right then hit a low bridge abutment head on. Harry moaned.

The engine hissed but had stopped running, pushed back against the firewall by the impact. The dashboard was crumpled, the steering wheel inches from Antoine's chest, the front window cracked and mostly gone. The night air floated into the car, damp and oppressive mixing with the smell of gasoline from the tipped gas can in the back seat that stung Antoine's nostrils.

"Can you move?" Antoine asked Harry. Harry worked to open the door.

"Get out!" Antoine said. Antoine's door was crushed and he slid out Harry's side.

He could not let the kid be found, or any evidence remain in the car. "Run" he said. He reached in his pocket, lit a lighter, and threw it in the back seat. There was a burst of flame. He pushed Harry. "Run. It'll blow."

"The key." Harry said. "The kid."

"Leave her!" Antoine said. But the keys were to many locks and could be evidence and they were in his hand. He slipped them in his pocket. "It's going to blow."

Antoine started running.

Harry went to the trunk pulling up on the lid. Nothing budged. He kicked, once, twice, three times. Fire flared in the open doors. Finally the trunk lid rose. Harry grabbed Suchin, her skin pale, her eyes shut.

Antoine was thirty yards away. The explosion, loud enough to hurt the ears, shot flames above the trees into the night sky. Metal and glass propelled with bullet speed. Harry didn't stop running, Suchin cradled in his arms. The clothes on his back burst into flame. His right carotid artery had been severed by a piece of glass that still glinted on the side of his neck, he stumbled on, finally falling forward. Suchin hit the ground face first. Harry fell just behind her.

Antoine reached Harry in seconds and stomped out the few burning cloth fragments that remained. Then he rolled his cousin over. He was breathing.

Harry coughed on his own blood. His eyes opened. "She okay?" he asked.

Antoine swore. The flames threw flickering shadows on his face and pinpoint, wiggling reflections glowed on his eyes.

Antoine turned Suchin over. She'd been dead a while, he could tell from the bloodless facial wounds on her face.

"Antoine," Harry gasped, "She okay?"

"She'll make it."

"You take care of her."

"Sure, man."

Despite the burning glow on his skin from the fire, Antoine shivered. He crossed himself.

Harry stopped breathing; the fire died in his eyes; the spirit shimmered out of him.

God bless you, you big dumb gorilla. The danger is in the caring—not the cops, or the FBI, or the syndicate. You cared too much. Like you ever listened.

Antoine knelt down and closed Harry's eyelids; he picked up the kid and tossed her into the flames of the Lincoln's burning trunk; then, as cars stopped and people were closing in from many directions, he blended into the dark to zigzag a course that would take him away from the city for a while.

Essays: The Art of Writing Literary Stories

Story: what to do

- Literary Fictional Story
- Character in Literary Fictional Story
- Narration of Literary Stories
- Drama
- Desire and Motivation
- Credibility
- Dialogue
- Improving Dialogue
- Characterization Improves Dialogue…
- Techniques for Excellence in Creating Character…
- How to Change Fiction Writing Style

Philosophy: write for the right reasons

- Author's Attitudes
- How Literary Stories Go Wrong
- Preparing to Write the Great Literary Story
- The Anatomy of a Wannabe Literary Fiction Writer
- Victims as Characters in Literary Fiction

Craft: do it well

- Momentum
- Information and Literary Story Structure
- 1st person POV in Literary Story
- Top Story/Bottom Story
- Strong Voice and Attention to Time
- Humor and Fiction
- Emotional Complexity in Literary Fiction
- Conflict in Literary Fiction

- What Exactly Is a Character-Based Plot?
- Writing in Scene: A Staple for Reader Engagement in Fiction
- Creating Story World (setting) in Literary Fiction
- Perception in Literary Fiction: A Challenge for Better Narration
- Creating Quality Characters in Literary Fiction
- Mastering the Power of a Literary Fictional Story
- Understanding Empathy
- Q & A On Learning to Think About Narration in Literary Fiction To Write Better Stories
- Incorporating Rhythm in Prose Style

Award-winning short stories by William H. Coles, read or listen online for FREE.

- A Simple Life
- Nemesis
- Gatemouth Willie Brown on Guitar
- The Wreck of the Amtrak's Silver Service
- The Indelible Myth
- Inside the Matryoshka
- Speaking of the Dead
- The Necklace
- The Golden Flute
- The Amish Girl
- Dr. Greiner's Day in Court
- The Cart Boy
- Big Gene
- Grief
- The War of the Flies
- Father Ryan
- The Gift
- Suchin's Escape

- The Stonecutter
- Facing Grace with Gloria
- Homunculus
- The Perennial Student
- The Activist
- Curse of a Lonely Heart
- The Miracle of Madame Villard
- On the Road to Yazoo City
- Captain Withers's Wife
- The Thirteen Nudes of Ernest Goings
- Reddog
- Clouds
- Dilemma
- Crossing Over
- The Bear
- Lost Papers
- Sister Carrie

NOVELS

- Tour of Duty
- McDowell
- Guardian of Deceit
- The Spirit of Want
- The Surgeon's Wife
- Sister Carrie

INTERVIEWS

- An Interview with Richard North Patterson.
- An Interview with Peter Ho Davies.
- An Interview with Tom Jenks.
- An Interview with Lan Samantha Chang.
- An Interview with Kirby Wilkins.
- An Interview with Josh Neufeld / Sari Wilson.
- An Interview with Jonathan Dee.
- An Interview with Fred Leebron.
- An Interview with Steve Almond.
- An Interview with Lee K. Abbott.
- An Interview with Robert Olen Butler.
- An Interview with Ron Carlson.
- An Interview with John Biguenet.
- An Interview with Jim Shepard.
- An Interview with Lee Martin.
- An Interview with David Lynn.
- An Interview with Michael Malone.
- An Interview with Michael Ray.
- An Interview with Susan Yeagley / Kevin Nealon.
- An Interview with Rebecca McClanahan.
- An Interview with Charles D'Ambrosio.
- An Interview with Rob Spillman.
- The Art of Creating Story
- Creating Literary Stories: A Fiction Writer's Guide

www.ingramcontent.com/pod-product-compliance
Lightning Source LLC
LaVergne TN
LVHW041945070526
838199LV00051BA/2912